Jessica slammed her bowl down on the table and stood up, her nose inches from Elizabeth's. "In this country people are innocent until proven guilty. If you were a little *smarter*, maybe you'd understand that."

Elizabeth narrowed her eyes. "I'm smart enough to know that you walked all over my hard work to get what you wanted. You know perfectly well that no one believes you could have gotten those scores without cheating," she yelled.

Jessica clenched her hands into fists. "So it's true!" she screamed. "Everyone, including my own twin, thinks I'm stupid. Well, you're going to discover otherwise when the truth finally comes out!"

Jessica glared at her sister, then turned on her heel and stalked out of the cafeteria.

SWEET VALLEY High

JESSICA THE GENIUS

Written by
Kate William

Created by
FRANCINE PASCAL

BANTAM BOOKS
NEW YORK · TORONTO · LONDON · SYDNEY · AUCKLAND

RL 6, age 12 and up

JESSICA THE GENIUS

A Bantam Book / September 1995

Sweet Valley High® *is a registered trademark of Francine Pascal*
Conceived by Francine Pascal
Produced by Daniel Weiss Associates, Inc.
33 West 17th Street
New York, NY 10011
Cover art by Bruce Emmett

ISBN: 0-553-56635-0

Published simultaneously in the United States and Canada

Bantam Books are published by Bantam Books, a division of Bantam
Doubleday Dell Publishing Group, Inc. Its trademark, consisting of the
words "Bantam Books" and the portrayal of a rooster, is Registered in
U.S. Patent and Trademark Office and in other countries. Marca
Registrada. Bantam Books, 1540 Broadway, New York, New York 10036.

PRINTED IN THE UNITED STATES OF AMERICA

OPM   0 9 8 7 6 5 4 3 2 1

To Nicole Pascal Johansson

Chapter 1

My entire future depends on this exam. Sixteen-year-old Elizabeth Wakefield sat hunched over the oak desk in her bedroom on Calico Drive. Sighing with frustration, she clutched her pencil so tightly, it broke in half.

Elizabeth leaned over and picked up the broken-pencil pieces from her off-white carpet. She gazed at her cluttered desktop. Usually, she liked to keep her desk impeccably neat, but now it was covered with math and English workbooks.

It was Friday night, and she was glued to her chair, studying for the SAT—the Standard Aptitude Test. Elizabeth sharpened a new pencil and turned to a fresh vocabulary list. She began copying words and committing them to memory. *Allude . . . antecedent . . . antediluvian . . .*

For several minutes the ticking of Elizabeth's clock

1

was the only sound in the room. She closed her eyes, trying to visualize the definition of "antediluvian."

"I have nothing to wear!" she suddenly heard Jessica yell from the hall. Elizabeth's door banged open and Jessica rushed into the room. She immediately headed toward Elizabeth's closet.

"Knocking is considered common courtesy in most civilized nations," Elizabeth commented dryly.

Conscientious . . . circumstantial . . .

"Knocking takes time, and time is of the essence," Jessica responded. She yanked open the louvered door of Elizabeth's closet. "I need to borrow some-thing—*fast*. Ken is picking me up in ten minutes."

"I can't believe you're even thinking about going out tonight." Elizabeth stared at her sister in disbelief.

Jessica pulled out a lavender silk tank top. "Why not? It's Friday." Jessica added the top to a growing pile on Elizabeth's bed.

"Jess, the SATs are tomorrow. You should be study-ing."

"You really are a nerd, Liz. Since when do I ruin my weekend with studying?" Jessica said, holding an embroidered denim shirt in front of her. "How does this look?"

"Let me repeat myself. The SAT—the exam that determines our entire college career—is tomorrow morning at eight o'clock."

"What's your point?" Jessica asked.

Elizabeth drummed her fingers on the desk. "My point is that our future is at stake. Don't you care?"

2

"Liz, I suggest you worry less about the future and enjoy the moment. It's called *joie de vivre*." Jessica leaned toward Elizabeth's full-length mirror, applying lipstick.

"You might wake up someday and realize that if you don't plan your future, you're going to end up with one that's not worth having." Elizabeth turned away from her twin and flipped the page of her workbook.

Jessica pulled on a black jacket over the denim top. "But no matter how much you plan, the unexpected always happens anyway. Right?"

"Sometimes you can expect the unexpected," Elizabeth said seriously. "But not always."

"Well, right now I expect to have dinner with my boyfriend at the Box Tree Cafe." Jessica arched an eyebrow at Elizabeth. "As for the next seventy years, I'm sure they'll turn out just fine."

"How can you be so confident?" Elizabeth asked, leaning back in her chair.

"I just know," Jessica responded lightly. "Don't I always get what I want, one way or another?" She turned and left the room, shutting the door behind her.

Elizabeth groaned with frustration. Although the rest of Sweet Valley High had been talking about nothing but the SATs for weeks, Jessica barely knew what the test was. And while Elizabeth had spent every afternoon of the last week taking a crowded preparatory class, Jessica had divided her time between the beach and the mall. *Typical*, Elizabeth thought, shaking her head.

Although the twins looked exactly the same, with turquoise-blue eyes, trim athletic figures, and silky blond hair, they couldn't have been more different. Elizabeth, who was four minutes older, was always considerate and hardworking. Her dream was to be a writer, and as a step toward that goal she wrote "Personal Profiles," a weekly column for *The Oracle*, Sweet Valley High's newspaper. Jessica, on the other hand, lived for fun, sun, and romance. She never thought more than five minutes ahead about anything.

Elizabeth gazed out her bedroom window, watching Jessica bound out of the house and jump into Ken Matthews's white Toyota. She slowly tapped her pencil on the desk and tried to concentrate on an algebra equation.

Elizabeth had worked too long and too hard to let Jessica's attitude affect her own drive. After years of getting straight-A's, she was going to make certain that the national college board knew she was an exceptional student. Then she could go to one of the best colleges in the country.

The highest possible score on the SATs was 800 in math and 800 in English. *And I'm going to get perfect scores on both test sections,* she promised herself. *I'll study all night if I have to.*

But what about Jessica? If her twin sister couldn't get into a prominent university, would Elizabeth just abandon her after they graduated from high school next year? Jessica thought she'd always be able to get what she wanted, but what did she know about the real world?

4

For both our sakes, I hope Jessica decides to get serious about her life, Elizabeth thought gloomily.

Todd leaned back in his desk chair and yawned. *Don't fall asleep,* he commanded himself. The numbers changed on his digital clock: 9:00 P.M. He'd been studying hard for the SATs since he'd walked in the door from basketball practice.

Time for a short break, he thought, stretching his arms. He reached for the unopened mail he'd tossed onto his bed that afternoon.

He'd received a postcard from a schoolmate back in Vermont, a note from his grandmother, and a newsletter from an athletic association. Then an envelope dropped into his lap from the University of Michigan. Todd frowned, puzzled. He didn't know anyone at the U of M. Who would have sent him a letter?

Todd ripped open the envelope and scanned the page inside. His eyes widened in shock and his jaw nearly fell into his lap. He blinked. Was he dreaming? He carefully read the letter again, soaking in each astonishing word:

Dear Todd,
    It is our pleasure to inform you that the University of Michigan is very impressed with your combined academic and athletic records. Our basketball scout has seen what you can do on the court, and he has highly recommended we recruit you for the University of Michigan

team. We boast one of the highest-ranking teams in the NCAA.

If we like you on the court as much as we expect to, we may be able to offer you a full basketball scholarship for your entire four years of college. There is one condition, however. In order to qualify for the scholarship, you must score above 600 on both sections of the SAT test. We wish you luck on the exam.

Sincerely,
Admissions Department,
University of Michigan

Todd stared at the letter, allowing the unbelievable words to sink in. A basketball scholarship! A jolt of energy swept through his body, completely melting his fatigue. Could this really be happening to him?

His heart pounded as he reread the letter. His gaze lingered on the last few lines. *You must score above 600 on both sections of the SAT.* He raked a hand through his dark-brown hair. That was a pretty high score.

Todd took a deep breath and clenched his fist. He was absolutely determined to get those scores. Nothing in the world had ever been so important.

Nothing except Elizabeth, he thought. He glanced at the framed photograph on his desk. Todd never ceased to be amazed by the incredible, beautiful girl who'd stood by him through so much.

Todd slammed shut his workbook. He had to see Elizabeth that night. They would celebrate his good news together.

Elizabeth opened her window and breathed in the sweet scent of freshly cut grass. Outside, it was a beautiful southern-California night. A light breeze ruffled her hair as she looked up at the star-filled sky.

Suddenly Elizabeth's heart-shaped face lit up. Todd was pulling his BMW into the Wakefield driveway.

When he climbed out of the car, Elizabeth leaned farther out the window so she could call to him. "Just come on in," she yelled.

She stepped into the hallway outside her bedroom door and watched him bound up the stairs. "I didn't expect to see you until tomorrow," she said, her sparkling blue eyes filled with love.

"I had to see you tonight," Todd said. He lifted her off the carpet in a bear hug.

"Somehow, I never get tired of hearing you say things like that," she laughed.

His lips brushed against hers and he held her tightly. Elizabeth hugged him back, savoring the warmth of his body. After a long moment, he tilted her chin up with one hand and looked into her eyes.

"Liz, everything I've ever wanted is coming together."

Elizabeth withdrew from the embrace and placed a hand lightly on Todd's arm. She led him into her

7

room. "What's going on?" she asked, pulling her bedroom door shut.

Todd threw off his letterman's jacket and tossed it onto a chair. Then he took both of Elizabeth's hands in his. "The University of Michigan has offered me a basketball scholarship," he said slowly.

Elizabeth gasped and her eyes widened. "Todd, that's incredible!" She threw her arms around his neck and held him closely. "I'm so proud of you," she whispered.

"Liz, if the University of Michigan wants me so much, maybe I'll get more offers from other places." His warm coffee-brown eyes shone brightly.

"Then we could choose which university would be best for both of us," Elizabeth said excitedly.

"Won't it be great when we're in college together?" Todd said, pulling her toward him for another embrace.

Elizabeth nodded. "Just imagine. There won't be anyone waiting up for us," she said quietly.

Todd bent his head and kissed her hair, her throat, and finally her lips. The kiss deepened, and she felt his strong arms wrap around her, drawing her closer to his strong body.

Finally, Elizabeth pushed him back. "Well, for the time being, my parents are still just a floor away."

"I see," Todd murmured, kissing her neck.

"I'm not kidding," Elizabeth giggled. "And besides, we both need to get back to the books."

He tenderly caressed her cheek. "I suppose

you're right. Michigan said I have to score over six hundred on the SATs to qualify for the scholarship."

"Piece of cake." Elizabeth smiled, her arms clasped around his waist.

Todd grinned and kissed her cheek. "Don't study too late, Liz. I'm picking you up early."

"I can't sleep. I'm too nervous," Elizabeth said, pulling away from Todd. She felt a sudden chill and wrapped her arms across her chest.

"You have nothing to be worried about—you're a genius," he said, kissing her forehead. Todd took her face in his hands and lightly touched her full lips with his fingertips. "Our lives together are just beginning. Now, go to sleep and dream about the future."

Saturday morning Elizabeth stumbled into the kitchen at seven thirty A.M. She tripped over Prince Albert, the Wakefield's golden retriever, who gave a small yelp when she stepped on his foot.

"Sorry, Albert," Elizabeth said with a sigh, scratching him behind the ears. "I had a rough night."

Elizabeth had stayed up studying until midnight, then tossed and turned for hours. She hadn't actually drifted off until four or five o'clock in the morning. Now she was so nervous and exhausted, her stomach felt as if an army were marching through it.

"You look like a train wreck, Liz," Jessica observed cheerfully. She was sitting at the kitchen table, and she looked wide-awake. Jessica leisurely munched cereal, reading the back of the box.

9

"Thanks, Jess," Elizabeth said irritably, slumping into a chair. She poured herself a cup of coffee. "Have you seen my keys?" she asked as she peered under a few papers on the table.

"I think Prince Albert had them for breakfast." Jessica put aside the cereal box and started reading the milk carton instead.

"Very funny," Elizabeth said. She leafed through a pile of mail.

Giving up on her keys, Elizabeth pulled the rubber band off the unopened newspaper next to Jessica. She scanned the headlines and distractedly tossed the paper down again.

"You can probably stop cramming. I doubt they'll ask about today's front page on the SATs."

"Laugh while you can," Elizabeth said, glowering. She rapped her fingers on the table. "I wish I could remember where I put my keys. My head feels like a sieve."

"Try some of this cereal," Jessica offered. "Pure sugar. Good brain food."

"No time for breakfast," Elizabeth responded. "Todd's picking me up in about one minute to drive to school for the—my keys are on the counter! How did they get there?"

"Admit it, your mind has turned into a swamp of vocabulary and math problems," Jessica said. "All practical information has sunk to the bottom."

A car honked in the driveway.

"I've got to run." Elizabeth grabbed her keys and

pulled on her jacket. "You'd better hurry up, too, or you'll be late."

"I can take care of myself, which is more than I can say for you," Jessica remarked. She walked to the refrigerator and took out a carton of orange juice.

"I hope you still feel that way when we get the test results back," Elizabeth said. She checked in her purse to make sure she had two number-2 pencils.

"You better bring a pillow to the test. You look like you're going to pass out in the middle of it," Jessica commented, stretching languorously.

"Thanks for the advice," Elizabeth said testily.

"Anytime." Jessica stood up and sauntered toward the stairs. As usual, she left the cereal box open and her breakfast dishes strewn around the table.

Elizabeth shook her head, then slung her purse over her shoulder. As she turned to leave the kitchen, she caught sight of herself in the glass oven door.

She had to admit that she did look tired—and she saw that she'd forgotten to brush her hair. Elizabeth quickly pulled a comb from her purse and ran it through her snarled blond mane.

"Get a grip," she whispered firmly to her reflection. Then she ran toward the front door. Todd was waiting.

The click of the test proctor's heels echoed on the linoleum classroom floor. In tense silence, rows of Sweet Valley High juniors and seniors sat bent over their SAT tests. Elizabeth wiped a bead of sweat from

11

her forehead and tried to keep focused. Unfortunately, her head felt as if it were stuffed with cotton.

She glanced up at the clock. It was eight twenty A.M. For a moment Elizabeth watched the other students furiously filling in answer boxes. Then she forced herself to turn back to her own test. But as she resumed reading questions, a sudden chill gripped her spine. She took another slow look at the people concentrating intensely all around her.

Where's Jessica?

Just then the door opened. Its loud squeak sliced through the atmosphere in the classroom. Jessica casually strolled in, smacking a piece of chewing gum. Seeing her, Elizabeth quietly clapped a hand to her forehead. *My sister has oatmeal for brains,* she groaned inwardly.

Elizabeth caught Jessica's eye and pointed at the clock. Jessica glanced at the time, then turned back to her sister and shrugged. She walked up to the proctor's table.

The proctor eyed Jessica disapprovingly and handed her the test materials.

"I don't have a pencil," Jessica said loudly. She blew a huge bubble, popped it, and sucked the gum back into her mouth.

"Shhhh!" whispered the proctor. "People are trying to concentrate." She handed Jessica a sharpened pencil.

Jessica gave her a big smile. "Thanks."

"No gum chewing is permitted during testing," the

proctor whispered sternly. "Spit it out and get to work."

Elizabeth momentarily squeezed her eyes shut and took a deep breath. Why didn't Jessica just sit down and stop making a spectacle of herself? At this rate, she was going to score about a negative fifty on the SATs.

When Jessica dumped her gum into the trash, it made a loud thud as it hit the bottom of the metal container. Elizabeth gripped her head with both hands.

Unzipping her jacket, Jessica slouched into a chair. Elizabeth glanced around the room and saw people shift in their seats. She wanted to wring her sister's neck for disturbing the other test takers. And how could anyone in her right *mind* show up *late* for this exam?

Elizabeth was shaking her head as she heard the sound of the second hand click across the clock face on the wall. Eight minutes had passed. A jolt of fear ran through Elizabeth as she realized that time was rapidly slipping away.

I have to concentrate.

She willed herself to focus her attention back on her own test. Logic problems and literary analogies swirled before her eyes. Jessica might not care about doing well on the SATs, but Elizabeth had worked her whole life to get to this point. She was determined to do better on this test than she'd ever done on anything.

Chapter 2

"I still don't understand why everyone is so wired over the SATs. It's just a test," Jessica said with disgust. "Can't anyone at this party talk about something more interesting—like Jamie Peters's new CD?"

She poured herself some punch from a crystal bowl and surveyed the crowded living room at Fowler Crest. It was Saturday night, and Lila Fowler was throwing a huge post-SAT party in her palatial, Spanish-style mansion in Sweet Valley's exclusive hill section.

"Only nerds would go to a hot party and talk about nothing but an exam," Amy Sutton agreed. She accepted a salmon-puff pastry from a white-jacketed waiter.

"Only a nerd would even score high on that ridiculous test," Lila said in a tone of boredom.

Jessica leaned casually against the marble refreshment table. "You said it. I forgot all about the SATs the second I turned in my test and walked out the door."

"Well, at least the SATs make a good excuse for a party," Lila said, running her fingers through her silky chestnut hair.

In her low-cut red top, short matching skirt, and sleek black cowboy boots, Lila looked as great as she always did. But Jessica secretly knew *she* looked even better in her black spaghetti-strap minidress, black stockings, and hammered gold earrings. Lila had long been Jessica's biggest rival, as well as her best friend.

"Let's go outside, you guys," Lila said to Jessica and Amy. "There's more action out there, even if the conversation isn't more stimulating."

Cars spilled out of the circular Fowler Crest driveway, and people were parking in the street at the edge of the Fowler property. Jessica waved to Bill Chase and DeeDee Gordon as they stepped out of Bill's car.

"Can you believe how crowded this place is?" Amy called to Bill and DeeDee.

"I think everyone in the junior class is here," DeeDee called back.

Lila pulled Jessica's arm. "Let's go out back where we can hear the music better." Lila was craning her neck as if she was looking for someone.

"Maybe some tall, dark, handsome stranger has crashed your party," Jessica suggested. "And he's dying to dance with you."

"My thoughts exactly."

Stereo speakers blasted music onto the back

15

patio. In the background the Fowler's large pool glowed with soft blue lights. Jessica looked around the backyard, absorbing the scene.

On the patio Dana Larson, the lead singer of Sweet Valley's best local band, The Droids, was dancing wildly with the other members of the band. She was dressed in one of her signature outfits—a green tunic with a black leather belt, purple tights over her long, slender legs, and black high-heeled boots.

"You look like you're having fun, Dana!" Kirk Anderson yelled.

"I am! I love partying like crazy after a big test!"

"If you ask me, this party's too tame!" Kirk responded.

"I agree!" Danny Porter yelled.

Suddenly Danny tore off his shirt and cannonballed into the shimmering swimming pool. Kirk dived in after him. The huge splash he made was followed by about ten other people's.

"Whoever cleans your pool is going to have his work cut out for him tomorrow, Li," Jessica observed.

"Who cares about tomorrow? I like to see people having a good time in the present moment." Lila smiled wryly. "That's what life is all about."

Jessica smiled back. "My thoughts exactly."

"Great party, Lila," Maria Santelli said, appearing with a plate of barbecued chicken and salad.

"Ah, but wasn't that invigorating, taking the SATs?" Winston Egbert said, appearing behind Maria. He put his arm around his girlfriend. "I could do it every

16

Saturday morning, just to get the blood flowing." He took his arm from Maria's shoulders and pounded his chest with one hand, while waving a chicken drumstick with the other. With his tall, lanky frame and unruly hair, Winston looked extremely ridiculous. Maria giggled, and Jessica rolled her eyes at Lila.

"You are truly the most amazing geek I have ever seen, Winston," Amy said, shaking her head incredulously.

"Thank you, thank you," Winston said, taking a deep bow. "But, Lila, I hope you won't stop writing me love letters after we leave Sweet Valley to attend famous universities."

Jessica and Amy laughed as Lila gave Winston a smoldering look.

"You'll have to excuse him," Maria said. "He's a little overstimulated. Too much caffeine." She arched an eyebrow and gave Winston an affectionate punch on the arm.

"But, seriously, I hope we'll all keep in touch after we graduate from the old jailhouse," Winston said. He pulled Maria close to him and kissed her on the cheek.

"I'll drink to that," Barry Rork added. He came up behind Amy and wrapped his arms around her waist. "How does everybody think they did today on the test?"

"Barry, can we *please* talk about something *else?*" Jessica groaned. "How to improve your golf game, ten ways to win at bingo—*anything* but the SATs."

17

"I don't know, I think the SATs are a pretty exciting subject," Barry said, shrugging toward Winston, who shrugged back.

"I've had it," Jessica said, throwing up her arms. "I need another glass of punch and a change of scenery."

Jessica strolled into the Fowler living room, weaving through people to find a quiet place alone. Everyone was being so boring, babbling on about the tests and college. She poured herself more punch and then leaned against the arm of a beige couch.

The room was expensively decorated in fine Southwest paintings and carvings. On the table next to Jessica was a bronze sculpture of a Native American, riding bareback on an Appaloosa, his long straight hair flying in the wind. Jessica rested an elbow on the sculpture. She imagined the muscular rider reaching out a powerful arm and lifting her beside him onto the back of the horse.

Just then she felt strong arms encircle her.

"How come you're hiding back here?" Ken asked softly. Jessica turned around and melted into his embrace. A moment later she felt his lips on her forehead.

"The SATs are occupying every square inch of everyone's brain," Jessica said. "And I'm sick of it." She rested her head on his chest.

"Well, getting into college is important to most people." Ken ran his fingers through her long silky hair.

"Don't remind me," Jessica sighed.

Ken playfully nibbled her ear. "By the way, have

you given any thought to what will happen if you've blown this exam and can't get into college?"

Clasping her hands around Ken's strong, athletic body, Jessica leaned back and gazed into his concerned blue eyes. "As a matter of fact, no. And I don't intend to."

Elizabeth sat slumped like a rag doll in a soft leather armchair in the Fowlers' comfortable den. Her eyes were closed, and she was on the verge of drifting into sleep.

"Looks like the SATs have just about killed your sister," she heard someone say through the haze of fatigue. It sounded like Bruce Patman's voice.

"Who knows?" Jessica said quietly. "They may have." Elizabeth opened her eyes and looked up to see Jessica perched on the arm of the leather chair.

"Hmmm, the patient is apparently still breathing," Bruce said. "I'll change my diagnosis from 'death' to 'total burnout.'"

"Can't a person find a peaceful corner to space out in?" Elizabeth put both hands on the chair arms and stiffly hoisted herself to an upright sitting position.

Dana Larson and DeeDee Gordon walked over, holding glasses of sparkling cider.

"You look like you could stand to lie on a Hawaiian beach for about a week," Dana said.

Jessica leaned her elbow on one thigh and placed her chin in the palm of her hand. "Life of the party, aren't you, Liz?" She asked dryly. "Studying like a

19

maniac for the SATs has turned you into a mummy."

"By the way, Jessica, that was quite a show you put on this morning," Bruce said casually as he pulled up an upholstered desk chair and sat down. He stretched his feet out on the floor in front of him and placed his hands behind his head. "Coming in late, forgetting pencils when we were explicitly asked to bring them, making enough noise to wake the dead—"

"Why are you of all people so concerned about the SATs?" Jessica interrupted. "You've got a guaranteed job in your father's business with or without those dumb exams."

Bruce Patman came from one of the richest families in Sweet Valley, and he never let anyone forget it. Bruce loved to show off his wealth by cruising around town in his black Porsche. He was also one of the best-looking—and most arrogant—guys at Sweet Valley High.

Bruce stiffened. "I'm still planning to go back east to an Ivy League college. And who knows what I'll eventually end up doing? Maybe I'll go into law."

"Maybe you'll go into medicine. You did an impressive job just now of diagnosing Elizabeth as not dead."

"What's this about Patman becoming a doctor?" Bill Chase asked, joining the group with Aaron Dallas.

"Maybe medicine," Bruce said evenly. He glared straight at Jessica with cold eyes. "Maybe I'll go to Wall Street and forget Sweet Valley ever existed."

"Yeah, right. I bet you never get out of Sweet

Valley," Jessica said, brushing a speck of lint off her skirt.

"What's that supposed to mean?" Bruce shot back. Aaron, Bill, and Dana all glanced at each other and at Kirk Anderson and Andrea Slade, who were wandering over with curious looks on their faces.

Elizabeth looked back and forth between Jessica and Bruce. She knew from experience that this exchange could quickly turn into a public brawl.

"You guys, maybe we *are* being a little too serious about this." All Elizabeth really wanted to do was stay clear of all warfare, go home, and crawl into bed.

"At least I have real dreams and serious goals," Bruce spit out, ignoring Elizabeth. He leaned forward in his chair, the muscles in his back tensed. "What do *you* have, Jessica? Are you planning to be a professional cheerleader?"

"Maybe I am," Jessica said in a low voice. She narrowed her eyes and glared at Bruce.

"Wakefield, you get more pathetic every day," Bruce said.

"Knock it off, you two, before this gets out of hand," Elizabeth finally said with as much energy as she could muster.

"Oh, your sister and I understand each other," Bruce said. He relaxed back in his chair and stared menacingly at Jessica. "It's just that she's naive and unsophisticated. She has no comprehension of the importance of the SATs."

"Well, what if she doesn't?" Elizabeth agreed wearily.

21

Jessica stood up and glanced angrily at Elizabeth and Bruce. "Aren't you two being just a little superior?" She stormed off.

Bruce watched her narrowly. Then his face reddened as he glanced quickly at the crowd of people drawn by the argument. He roughly pushed the chair aside and walked away.

Elizabeth turned her gaze from Bruce, and her eyes searched among the milling party-goers for Jessica. She finally caught sight of her twin pushing her way through the crowd and stalking out of the living room.

Elizabeth limply threw up her hands, then dropped them with resignation on the arms of the plush chair. She'd given up caring about Jessica's future. She had her own to worry about.

As Elizabeth leaned back in the large, warm chair, she caught sight of Todd laughing with Aaron. She closed her eyes and imagined sitting with Todd in a sailboat on the Charles River, near Harvard University, at the start of their freshman year. In the vision Todd pulled her close to him, and she traced the large black *H* embossed on his crimson sweater.

"From now on, it's clear sailing, Liz," she heard him whisper.

She smiled as she fell asleep. Nothing could possibly stand in the way of her dream.

Chapter 3

Four weeks later . . .

Jessica sat lazily at the kitchen table on a Monday afternoon. She was dressed in her favorite electric-blue bikini and was trying to select from an array of suntan oils. *Should I go for coconut or avocado?* she wondered.

As she reached for the coconut oil, she spied two envelopes sandwiched between a salt shaker and an embroidered napkin holder. One was for her, and one for Elizabeth. The return address on each said "Princeton Educational Testing Service—SAT Division."

Not the SATs again, Jessica thought, rolling her eyes. In the weeks since they'd taken the test, Jessica had forgotten about it completely. She opened her envelope, scanned the contents, and tossed the piece of paper back onto the table.

She glanced at the clock. Lila was meeting her at

the Valley Mall in an hour, and Jessica wanted to get some sun before facing the rigors of trying on clothes. She flung a towel over her shoulder and grabbed the dark bottle of coconut oil.

As Jessica opened the sliding glass door that led to the Wakefields' swimming pool, she hesitated a moment. Had she read that letter right?

Stepping back to the table, she picked up the thin piece of paper and looked it over again, furrowing her brow. A strange shock ran through her body. She wasn't exactly sure how these things were graded, but she'd heard Elizabeth discuss the test enough to have a vague idea about what was a good score. Weren't her numbers kind of high?

Jessica sat back down at the table, staring at her score sheet. She'd done well on the SATs. Really well. She hadn't exactly run herself into the ground studying for the stupid test—so how could she have aced it?

Jessica shrugged. She'd been so bored with everyone talking about the SATs, she wasn't about to waste time contemplating how she'd managed to pull off these scores.

Suddenly Jessica stiffened as she remembered what Lila had said at her post-SAT party.

Only a nerd would score high on that ridiculous test.

Was Jessica a nerd in hip clothes? She shuddered—that would be a fate worse than death. Nerds were geeks like Winston Egbert, and if people at Sweet Valley High found out about her SATs, they might actually *associate* her with Winston.

Jessica slipped the paper back into the envelope and set it down on the table. These scores were incredibly embarrassing.

Well, no one had to find out about her scores, did they? Jessica squared her shoulders and wrapped her towel around her waist. She picked up a bottle of aloe vera from the table, just to steady the shaking in her hand.

"Jess, our SAT scores must have arrived. Enid got hers today!" Elizabeth yelled as she flew into the kitchen.

She dumped her school books onto the table—then caught sight of a letter from ETS, Educational Testing Service, with her name on it.

She grabbed the letter with both hands. "What are you doing just standing there with a bottle of lotion in your hand?" she demanded. "Aren't you curious?"

"I'm desperate with curiosity, can't you tell?" Jessica answered, setting down the bottle. "But more important, I'm hungry." She walked to the refrigerator, took out a melon, and placed it on the cutting board.

"How can you eat at a time like this?" Elizabeth held up her envelope like a trophy. She was so excited she could hardly breathe. "I've got dibs on using the phone this afternoon. I'm going to have to call Todd. And Enid—she scored six-seventy verbal and six-fifty math."

"That's the most exciting news I've heard all week," Jessica said flatly as she sliced into the fruit.

Elizabeth arched an eyebrow. "If I didn't know better, I'd say you were jealous."

"I don't think so," Jessica responded coolly.

"For once, Jess, maybe you'll see how hard work and preparation really pay off." Elizabeth took a deep breath and ripped open her letter.

I hope, hope, hope I got a perfect score. She read her score report and gasped.

"Good news?" Jessica asked, cutting the melon into cubes.

Elizabeth said nothing. Instead, she clutched the top of a kitchen chair to steady herself, feeling as if she were plummeting through space from the top of a thirty-story building. She didn't get a perfect score—far from it.

With math and verbal combined, she hadn't broken 1000. That was much less than she'd expected.

Elizabeth stared at the numbers, her body slowly freezing into a solid block of ice. Then she noticed Jessica's open letter and envelope lying on the table.

"Mind if I take a look?" Elizabeth asked in a whisper.

"Go ahead," Jessica said, glancing over her shoulder. She waved her paring knife at Elizabeth. "Just don't tell anyone."

Elizabeth picked up the paper and read Jessica's SAT scores. She nearly choked. Jessica had scored 760 in verbal and 750 in math!

"There must be some mistake!" Elizabeth wailed.

"What are you talking about?" Jessica asked. She

leaned against the counter, eating melon chunks with her fingers.

"The test, our scores! They must have got us mixed up!" Elizabeth shrieked in exasperation.

Jessica shrugged. "So what? It's just a bunch of numbers." She took her bowl of fruit in one hand, a bottle of coconut oil in the other, and headed toward the back door.

Elizabeth lowered herself into a kitchen chair and laid her trembling palms facedown on the table. She was too shocked to cry. She'd studied so incredibly hard for that exam. In fact, she'd studied hard all her life, in every class she ever took. So how could she have done this horribly on the SATs?

She'd never get into a good college now. Her dream of going to Harvard was crushed into a heap of rubble, like fine china smashed on sharp rocks.

And how could she face people in school tomorrow? Everyone in the junior and senior classes at Sweet Valley High would be talking about their SAT scores. She couldn't possibly tell anyone what she got.

"I can't believe how late it is. I only have thirty minutes for tanning," Jessica complained as she slid open the glass door.

Elizabeth stared at her sister. "How can you be so casual, Jessica?" she said slowly. "How do you manage to just sail through life like this?"

"Oh, I have my ways," Jessica said with a wave of her hand. She stepped outside and shut the door.

Elizabeth's glazed stare moved to the mess Jessica had left on the counter. The ripped-open melon, with its guts smeared all over the wooden cutting board, looked exactly the way Elizabeth felt.

Chapter 4

"I like the feel of this fabric. What do you think?" Lila asked as she modeled a strapless emerald-green dress.

"Nice," Jessica said. "That color really accentuates your eyes." She stood with one hand on her hip and nodded with approval at Lila's choice.

Jessica and Lila had been checking out stores for a couple of hours. First they'd wandered into Blue Parrot Crafts to look at tie-dyed T-shirts, then into Foxy Mama to browse the tight jeans and leather jackets. Now they were in Lisette's. Lila was interested in serious shopping, and Lisette's was one of the most expensive boutiques in the Valley Mall.

"I love having a little extra spending money at my disposal," Lila murmured. She ran her hands down the smooth sides of the slinky dress. "That's the best part of getting those idiotic exams out of the way."

"Why? Is your time freed up now to rob banks?"

"Not quite," Lila said, turning to see how the dress looked from the back. "My father offered me more shopping money than usual if I scored in the five hundreds on the SATs—which, of course, I did."

"Anything to further the noble cause of fashion," Jessica said. She should have known it would be impossible to go anywhere in Sweet Valley without someone bringing up the irritating subject of the SATs. Even Lila was obsessed.

"Anything to get him off my back about schoolwork and onto the more satisfying subject of cash," Lila responded.

"Mmm," Jessica said. She held a peacock-blue silk top to her chest. At least this conversation was veering back to the right topic—the subject of buying clothes.

"My father's been doing nothing but lecturing me on how important it is to do well on college-entrance exams," Lila said, running her fingers over the other dresses draped on their hangers in the fitting room.

"What a drag," Jessica said. *We've got to get off this subject, and fast.*

"I'll say. It's not like I'm going to his alma mater, Yale, anyway," Lila said.

"What? And pass up the chance to join the chess club with Winston Egbert?" Jessica asked, taking advantage of an opportunity to shift topics. Talking about guys was just as safe as talking about fashion.

"I'd rather wear polyester," Lila said dryly. "No, I

have big plans to stay right here and go to Sweet Valley University. There's no way I'm getting too far from the best beaches and malls in the world—not to mention the best-looking guys." Lila twirled so that the emerald skirt flared out from her body.

Jessica said nothing. She had pulled on the peacock-blue top and matching silk pants and was contemplating her reflection. Lila stopped twirling and stared into the mirror with lowered lids.

"That's perfect for you, Jess," Lila said. "You should definitely start wearing more silk."

"Think I should get it?" Jessica asked. She adjusted the three-way mirror so that she could look at herself from all angles.

"Of course you should get it," Lila exclaimed. "It'll be you and me, Jess, catching the attention of every upper-class guy on the volleyball and swim teams at SVU."

Jessica grinned. "Lila, are you actually offering to share your men with me? What's come over you?"

"I just happen to know that you and I are the hottest, most alluring team at Sweet Valley High," Lila said. She adjusted the square collar on Jessica's jewel-blue shirt.

"I won't argue with that," Jessica agreed.

Lila tossed her thick dark hair. "And I only associate with the coolest people at school. I have a reputation to uphold, don't I?"

Jessica smiled.

"Wow, it's getting late," Lila said, glancing at her

gold-and-diamond wristwatch. "I have to get home. Robby is picking me up in forty-five minutes. We're going to an art-gallery opening."

They got back into their jeans and boots and left the dressing-room area. As Jessica flipped one last time through the racks of chic clothing, she noticed with satisfaction the number of patrons and clerks who turned their heads to stare at her.

"I think they're looking at us," Jessica whispered, nudging Lila.

"They should be," Lila said.

Jessica liked the way people looked at her. It was true that the combination of Jessica and Lila, either in jeans and T-shirts or dressed to kill on a Saturday night, set Sweet Valley on fire.

And though Jessica would never admit it aloud in ten million years, she liked being part of Lila Fowler's coveted inner circle. Nothing was going to interfere with Jessica's reputation for being gorgeous, fashionable, and too cool to care about school.

"By the way, Jess, how did you do on the SATs?" Lila asked casually. She pulled a blazing-red tunic made of hand-washable silk from the rack and checked the price tag.

Jessica froze in her tracks, lightly clutching to her chest the blue outfit she'd tried on.

"Well?" Lila asked expectantly, glancing up at Jessica. "You didn't do *that* bad, did you?"

Jessica had sworn not to tell anyone her real SAT scores. But she and Lila were good friends. And didn't your good friends accept you, no matter what? On the other hand, Lila's standards for coolness were strict. Nerds were out. If Jessica told the truth, would Lila laugh in her face?

"No, not that bad. Not great, but decent," Jessica mumbled, her stomach coiled like a spring. She pretended to be captivated by the wool fabric of a shirt imported from Ireland. She held her breath as she waited to see if Lila would ask for the actual scores.

"Hmmm, that's good," Lila said. She was reading the washing instructions on the inside collar of the red tunic. "I love this fabric, but I don't have time now to pick out a skirt to go with the tunic."

"Well, you can always come back," Jessica said quickly.

"You're right, let's go."

As they left the boutique and walked toward the parking lot, Jessica slowly let out her breath and felt her stomach unwind. Lila hadn't asked her scores. *Besides, she wouldn't really think I was a loser if she knew how high my scores were, would she?*

But a chill of doubt crept up Jessica's spine. What *would* people say if they found out she'd aced the SATs?

"You look great in that color, Jess," Ken said as he slid into the seat next to hers at Cafe Feliz.

Jessica flashed him a beautiful smile. "I thought you might like this outfit. I just got it today."

"Oh, right, that shopping spree you were headed

for with Lila." Ken shook his head, his eyes glowing. "The two of you are really something."

As the cool evening breeze blew through her hair, Jessica opened the menu and scanned the selection of fresh salads and gourmet burgers. They were sitting at one of the cafe's outdoor tables, which was canopied by a big striped umbrella. Ken's hand brushed against hers as he spread his own menu open on the heavy white tablecloth.

"You're really beautiful, Jessica," Ken said. He touched her fingers. "You're without a doubt the prettiest girl at Sweet Valley High. I've heard guys on the football team talking about your incredible looks when they thought I was out of earshot."

"That doesn't make you just a little bit jealous, does it?" Jessica said with a grin.

"No, Jess," he said quietly as he stroked his index finger along the back of her hand. "It makes me proud to know that the sexiest girl in school is my girlfriend."

Ken's words and the soft touch of his strong fingertips sent streaks of electricity through Jessica's limbs.

"Are you folks ready to order?"

Jessica glanced up into the face of the handsome dark-haired waiter. Smiling down at her, he stood poised with a pad of paper and a pen.

"Which do you recommend, the chef's salad or the Caesar salad? Or maybe a burger?" Jessica asked the waiter flirtatiously. She leaned an elbow on the table, resting her palm against her cheek, and gazed at him with her wide blue eyes.

"Uh, you might like a garden avocado burger," the waiter stammered.

Jessica smiled with satisfaction as he turned slightly red, then quickly scribbled something onto his pad. He must be captured under her spell, she thought. In fact, the owner of the restaurant was probably about to come over and say their meal was on the house, just because Jessica's presence had brightened up the restaurant so much.

"Mmm, that sounds delicious," Jessica responded. She stretched languorously and ran a hand through her hair.

"Get anything you want, Jess. This evening is totally on me," Ken said generously. "I feel like celebrating."

Jessica winked at the waiter. "OK, then let's go for it. A garden avocado burger, a vanilla milk shake, and an order of fries."

"I'll have the same," Ken said. He handed both menus to the waiter, then turned back to Jessica.

"I'd like a bottle of French mineral water to start," Jessica added. The waiter looked over Ken's head and into her eyes. "With a slice of lime." The young man smiled appreciatively at her, then turned and walked quickly toward the kitchen.

Jessica looked back at Ken, who clasped both her palms, then ran his fingers along her forearms.

"So why are you in such a good mood tonight?" Jessica asked. The moon had risen in the dark sky, and she watched the light dance across Ken's chiseled features. She was so filled with warmth just sitting

35

across the table from him, she felt she could almost float in the air like a helium balloon.

"I got really good scores on the SATs," he said proudly.

Not the SATs again. Jessica felt like a punctured tire, with the air suddenly rushing out. "That's great, Ken," she said, trying not to sound too deflated. She'd die of boredom if she had to endure one more conversation about the SATs, even with Ken. She slid her hand from his and idly fingered the salt shaker.

"I had to get five hundred or above on both sections to get into Sweet Valley University. I scored five-thirty on math and five-twenty on verbal, so I'm set," he said with excitement.

"That's great, Ken," Jessica repeated. She idly arranged packets of sugar into rows across the table.

"Everybody thought the SATs were really hard," Ken said. He sat back in his chair with a satisfied air. "But I didn't think so. I thought they were pretty easy."

"Are you still going to play football at SVU?" Jessica asked, trying to change the subject. "You can't study all the time, you know."

"I know. I've certainly learned that from you," Ken said with a grin. "Sure, I'll go out for the team," he added. "But it's the business courses I'm really looking forward to. I'm just so *stoked* about my scores."

"Well, I'm sure you'll have the time of your life at SVU," Jessica said. She absently unscrewed the cap on the ketchup bottle and then screwed it back on again.

"*We* will have the time of our lives, Jess.

Together," Ken said softly, reaching up and touching her face. "I'll still need to have the prettiest girl in the world by my side."

Jessica smiled and pushed the ketchup bottle aside. Now, *this* was a *much* more interesting topic. She looked deeply into Ken's brilliant blue eyes.

The waiter arrived and set down their drinks and french fries. Jessica kept her gaze focused on Ken as she lifted the glass of sparkling water to her lips.

"Hey, how did you end up doing on the SATs?" he asked.

"Oh, not that great," Jessica said with a shrug. She tipped her head back and took a long swallow of cool water.

"Well, I'm not too surprised, Jess," he said with a smile, his eyes crinkling at the corners. "It's not like anyone expected you to do really well. Don't take it hard, though. It's OK."

Jessica tipped her head to one side and watched Ken ask the waiter for another Coke. "Hey, I'm not *that* dumb," she said lightly, slowly setting her glass down on the table.

"I didn't say you were dumb. It's just that, you know . . ." Ken said.

"It's just that what?" Jessica asked.

The dark-haired waiter appeared and set their burgers down in front of them.

"I hope you find this cooked to your satisfaction," the handsome waiter said demurely to Jessica. She simply stared at Ken as he dug into his food.

"This is terrific. I was starving," Ken said with his mouth full. "Jessica, have some fries."

"You sound like you, um, expected me to do badly on the SATs," Jessica said, eyeing Ken. She took a small bite of her burger and put it back down on the plate while Ken continued to wolf down his dinner.

"Well, you know, doing really well on stuff related to school isn't your strong suit. Scholastics is more Elizabeth's department," Ken responded, rolling a french fry in the ketchup.

Jessica choked down another bite of burger. "Well, yeah, I don't really care about school. I never have. But that doesn't necessarily mean I'm not smart, does it?"

Ken took a sip of Coke. "Jess, everyone doesn't have to be smart in that way," he said sympathetically. "You've got plenty going for you."

Jessica wiped her mouth and then crushed the napkin in her lap. Of course she wanted Ken to be drawn to her lithe body and Pacific-blue eyes. But didn't he also love her for her quick mind and sharp wit? She didn't want to give Ken the impression that the SATs were any big deal to her. But she didn't want him to think she was stupid, either.

"Ken, listen, I want to tell you the truth," Jessica said, sitting up straighter in her chair. "I actually did really well on the SATs. I scored a seven-fifty in Math and a seven-sixty in English." Jessica took a long drink of her cold milk shake.

"Jessica, I said it doesn't matter. You don't have to

make stuff up." Ken laughed. "I love you for what you are and accept you for what you're not." He ate the last bite of his hamburger and pushed his chair back from the table.

"I guess I'm lucky to have a guy who's so understanding," Jessica said slowly.

Ken touched her lightly under her chin. "We're lucky to have each other."

Jessica stared down at her empty plate until a hand reached out and whisked it away. Despite the delicious meal, her stomach felt strangely hollow.

"Hey, Liz, are you that surprised that I did so well on the SATs?" Jessica asked on Tuesday morning. She threw her books into the backseat and slid into the Jeep next to Elizabeth.

"Well, I suppose it is kind of unexpected," Elizabeth said, her voice flat. She backed the Jeep out of the driveway and pulled onto Calico Drive.

"I mean, not that I care about the SATs, but does it seem strange that I might be smart?" Jessica asked.

Elizabeth winced. She opened the window and let warm wind fill the car. *Does it seem strange that I might not be smart?*

"Of course not. Why would you think that?" Elizabeth asked. She sighed. It was inevitable that everyone would be talking about the SATs that day. But she'd been hoping to avoid the subject until they actually got to school and there was nowhere to hide.

· "Oh, it's just that I hinted to Ken that I had low

scores, and he tried to make me feel better about not having a great brain," Jessica said offhandedly. "I guess he was just being nice."

Elizabeth glanced at Jessica out of the corner of her eye.

"Why didn't you tell him the truth?" Elizabeth asked. She turned right onto a palm-lined street.

"I finally did. He didn't believe me. But it's no big deal," Jessica responded vaguely. She shrugged, then looked out the window and casually twirled a strand of hair around her finger. But Elizabeth detected the note of hurt pride in her sister's voice.

Still, the SAT was the last thing Elizabeth wanted to discuss. Just the thought of her test scores made her feel like turning around and going back to bed. Heading toward school felt like facing an execution.

"Well, I'm sure he didn't mean whatever he said the way it must have come out," Elizabeth said wearily. "To tell you the truth, though, I don't feel like talking about the SATs right now."

"Yeah, me either," Jessica said. "The whole day in school will probably be totally annoying, with everyone asking everyone else what they scored."

Elizabeth felt her stomach twist. She turned left at the convenience store that was one block from school. When she saw the Sweet Valley High parking lot in the distance, she suddenly felt a twenty-pound weight on her shoulders.

"I mean, our scores are really no one else's business," Jessica continued.

"No, they're not, are they?" Elizabeth said thoughtfully. "In fact, they're a pretty private matter."

"Exactly," Jessica said. She sulkily folded her arms. "I'm not going to tell anyone my scores, even if they ask."

Elizabeth pulled the Jeep onto the blacktop student-parking area. As she turned off the engine, she decided to slide through the day without talking to anyone about the SATs. Just realizing she had that choice made her feel a tiny bit better.

Elizabeth opened the car door and glanced up at the school building—and her heart stopped.

"Oh, no! Look!" Jessica cried.

Hanging right above Sweet Valley High's front entrance was a banner printed in huge block letters.

"Congratulations, Jessica Wakefield and Winston Egbert—highest SAT scorers at Sweet Valley High," Elizabeth read hoarsely.

"My name is associated with Winston Egbert! I'm going to die of humiliation," Jessica said. She slid down in the car seat. "Don't tell anyone I'm here."

"Hey, there she is! Miss Nerd Queen, U.S.A.," someone yelled.

People rushed into the parking lot and flocked around the Jeep.

"Way to go, Wakefield," Barry said. He opened the car door and slapped Jessica on the back.

"So this is the *real* Wakefield brain," Aaron said. Elizabeth caught her breath and fought back a wave of tears.

41

Kirk shoved a pad of paper and a pen under Jessica's nose. "Can I have your autograph?"

A slow smile crept over Jessica's red face. "Well, I never turn down a request for an autograph." She dashed off her signature and handed the paper and pen back to Kirk, laughing flirtatiously.

"Let's go, Jess, you've got a big day ahead of you," Andrea said, dragging Jessica from the car.

Jessica grabbed the car door with one hand and the roof with the other. "No! I won't go!" she protested with a big grin.

"I'll give you a hand," Dan Scott offered. He peeled Jessica's fingers from the car door and helped Andrea pry her out of the Jeep.

"If you guys rip the material on my silk shirt, I expect you to fly to China and get me a new one just like it!" Jessica yelled, laughing so hard she almost couldn't stand up.

"It's a deal!" Andrea agreed.

Elizabeth watched Andrea and Dan pull Jessica by both arms through the parking lot and into the school building. Jessica laughed the whole way.

Claws of jealousy ripped at her insides. Elizabeth hated the nauseating envy she felt; she knew she should be happy for her sister, but she couldn't help feeling resentful. Jessica didn't care in the slightest about the SATs or getting into college. It was obvious that all she did care about was reveling in the spotlight.

How was it *possible* that Jessica had received the highest scores in the school, and Elizabeth had failed so miserably? It didn't make sense—something had to have gone wrong. Maybe the testing service *did* get their scores switched. Then again, maybe she was just plain stupid.

Elizabeth dragged herself toward the building, staring at the banner above the school's heavy front door. Everyone had followed Jessica inside, leaving the parking lot empty. A stray soda can rolled by Elizabeth in the silent breeze, and she kicked it angrily against a curb.

She felt her stoic resolve to avoid people all day melt into the asphalt, knowing she desperately needed to talk to someone. The one person who would understand her feelings and confusion was Todd. She had to find him. He would believe in her—no matter what.

Chapter 5

"Nice going, Jessica," Ricky Ordway said. He leaned across two seats in the school auditorium to give her a pat on the arm. Jessica was sitting next to Lila, with her feet propped up on the seat in front of her.

"It sure is noisy in here," Jessica said.

"It certainly is," Lila acknowledged, casting Jessica a sideways glance. "And every single conversation seems to be about you."

Jessica smiled to herself with satisfaction. Then she quickly replaced her smile with a look of boredom.

"When is Chrome Dome going to get here? I don't want this to take all day," Jessica complained. She scanned the auditorium, looking for Sweet Valley High's bald-headed principal.

"I don't know, but I think he means to honor you and your soul mate, Winston Egbert, *big*-time," Lila said.

"I can't believe I'll have to stand on that stage with Winston. Talk about an all-time low."

"So what's your secret?" Lila asked, arching an eyebrow. "Do you have any idea how much shopping money I'd be showered with if *I'd* scored in the seven hundreds?"

Jessica yawned. "Suntanning and fashion magazines. That's my tried-and-true secret of success."

"Hey, genius!" Bill Chase said, coming up behind Jessica. He shook her by the shoulders, rattling her head back and forth.

"Thanks for your enthusiasm, Bill," Jessica said dizzily. "But how about leaving my head on my shoulders?"

"I guess you'll need it for doing advanced calculus," he said.

Jessica turned around in her seat and surveyed the crowded room, catching Sandra Bacon giving her a thumbs-up. Jessica had to admit, she felt as if she were queen for a day. This must be what it was like to be famous. If so, she could get used to it pretty easily.

Just as she was turning back around, she spotted Bruce sitting two rows away, watching her grimly.

"What's the matter with Bruce?" she asked Lila. "He looks like he's trying to place a curse on me."

Lila pulled a nail file out of her purse. "Don't mind him, he's just jealous."

"Of what?" Jessica snorted. "Has he decided our Jeep is cooler than his black Porsche?"

"Didn't you hear? Bruce is bent out of shape because he scored low on the SATs," Lila answered confidentially.

"Is that right?" Jessica asked. She slowly turned to face Bruce. "He was pretty obnoxious to me at your party. And what goes around comes around—isn't that what they say?"

"They do say that," Lila said, examining herself in the mirror of her compact case.

"Hey, Bruce!" Jessica called. "Sorry you did a lousy job on the SATs! Still planning to trade Sweet Valley for the Ivy Leagues?"

Bruce turned red and stared hatefully at Jessica. Students in all the seats around him stopped their conversations.

"Watch your step, Wakefield," Bruce warned bitterly. "Life can take strange, unexpected turns for the worst."

"So how'd you do?" Todd asked Ken as he leaned back in his auditorium seat.

"Not bad, low five hundreds," Ken said quietly. His gaze seemed to be fixed on Jessica, who was sitting toward the front of the auditorium. "Good enough for SVU."

"That's great," Todd said distractedly. "I did awesome. I've never been so psyched in my life."

"Maybe this award assembly could have been for you," Ken said, looking down at his hands.

"I don't mind Winston and Jessica getting all the attention today." Todd placed his hands comfortably behind his head. "I've had a lot more successes in general than Winston."

Ken arched an eyebrow. "You sound awfully pleased with yourself. What's going on?"

"Well, the University of Michigan wants to recruit me for a full basketball scholarship," Todd answered modestly.

"No kidding," Ken said.

"No kidding," Todd responded with a broad grin. "Want to see the letter?"

Todd opened his notebook and pulled out the letter, his ticket to the future. He read it again to himself and, beaming, handed it to Ken. "Careful, it glows with so much praise, it's almost radioactive."

Ken shot a glance at Todd. Then he read the letter, lifting his eyebrows and whistling. "Impressive."

"I thought so," Todd said. He took a deep, satisfied breath. "They'll send a representative to watch the big game that's coming up next month, but that's just a formality. The hard part's over, now that I've aced the SATs."

"Yeah, well, I guess you've really got something to be proud of," Ken said tightly as he handed the letter back to Todd. "I hope it all works out for you."

"Piece of cake," Todd said with a shrug. He gingerly placed the letter back in his notebook.

Ken cleared his throat and shifted slightly away from him. Todd realized Ken was probably jealous. Why not? Todd was heading for the big time, leaving the tiny world of Sweet Valley behind.

He could already see his picture in the freshman catalog: Todd Wilkins, basketball championship scholar.

The school would probably post a blowup of his photograph in the dorm lobby, alongside pictures of other highly accomplished students and famous alumni.

"Here comes Chrome Dome," Ken announced, turning around in his seat.

The school principal walked through the auditorium door, carrying two plaques under his arm.

"Looks like the show's about to start," Todd said with a bored tone.

Ken turned sharply back to Todd. "You know, this probably is kind of a big deal for Jess and Winston."

"Sure, it's a nice little ceremony. Gives a couple of kids who haven't done that much their few minutes in the limelight," Todd answered.

"How generous of you, Todd," Ken said sarcastically. "You're starting to remind me of someone else I know rather well. I think it's Bruce Patman."

Todd laughed. He was hardly anything like Patman, who'd never worked hard enough to achieve something truly great.

"You know, we always figured Egbert would end up in some corner of an Ivy League library. But who would've thought Jessica would show up with those kind of brains?" Todd commented.

"Uhm, right, kind of an interesting twist," Ken stammered. He narrowed his eyes at Todd, then looked back toward the front of the auditorium. "I guess stranger things have happened."

Mr. Cooper stepped onto the stage and began testing the microphone. Todd yawned and closed his eyes. All he wanted to do was make it through the day and get to basketball practice.

He imagined himself at the big game next month, dribbling down the center of the court. People in the bleachers would applaud and scream cheers for him, while the other team scrambled unsuccessfully to block his lightning movements. He'd score the winning basket in the final moments of the game.

The Michigan recruiter would jump down from the stands and wrap a proud arm around Todd's shoulders. Suddenly representatives would appear from Harvard and Yale, begging Todd to accept their scholarships and play for their teams.

"You're a shooting star," each competing recruiter would whisper to him. "And I can take you to the moon."

"Good morning, everyone," Chrome Dome Cooper said. "And good morning, especially, to Jessica Wakefield and Winston Egbert." He cleared his throat.

Lila gave Jessica a light nudge. "You're on soon. I suggest you make this the performance of your life."

"Can I go onstage with a bag over my head?"

"No."

"As most of you know by now, Jessica and Winston have received the highest SAT scores in the junior class," Chrome Dome continued. "We are here this morning to honor them for their achievements."

"Way to go, Jessica," Ricky called, clapping loudly.

Danny let out a hoot, and Kirk whistled from the

49

back of the auditorium. Jessica rolled her eyes and buried her head in Lila's shoulder.

"The natives are restless," Lila said in a low voice.

"I've never been so embarrassed in my life," Jessica mumbled into her shoulder. "He said 'Jessica and Winston' as if we were a couple, or something."

Jessica sat up and looked around. She spotted Winston sitting next to Maria in the row ahead of her. He was looking up at Chrome Dome with an expression of reverence.

"Check out Winston. He looks like he's in church," Jessica said to Lila, cupping her hand to her mouth.

"I'm sure this is the peak moment of his life," Lila said dryly.

The microphone squealed a high-pitched sound, and a student technician ran out from backstage to adjust it. Chrome Dome pulled a handkerchief from the pocket of his brown jacket and mopped his glistening bald head.

Lila propped her fingers against her chin. "We have got to get that man into some decent clothes," she whispered, shaking her head.

"Can't you just see Chrome Dome in an Italian suit?" Jessica whispered back.

"And an Italian Fiat to go with it, in place of that brown Dodge Dart," Lila murmured.

"I'd like now to call Jessica and Winston to the stage to receive their awards," Chrome Dome's voice boomed over the loudspeaker.

"All *right*," Aaron yelled, raising a fist in the air.

Danny and Kirk stood up and applauded. Ricky shouted out, "Yes!" and made catcalls.

Winston stood in the aisle and grinned stupidly at Jessica, hooking his elbow in the air.

"He wants you to take his arm." Lila nudged Jessica. "Come on, this is your big chance for a date with Winston."

"I hate this! I can't go on that stage with him—my reputation will be ruined forever. I think I'm going to die," Jessica said. She covered her face with her hands.

"Well, die later. Right now, get up there and accept your award." Lila gave her a shove.

Jessica dragged herself into the aisle and marched up the stage steps with Winston.

"My lady hath both beauty *and* brains," Winston said, dramatically clutching at his heart.

"Back off, Egbert," Jessica hissed.

Jessica walked onto the stage and stood stiffly next to Winston, who kept inching closer to her.

"I am proud to present each of you with your own engraved plaque commemorating this outstanding achievement," Chrome Dome said.

"Thanks," Jessica said, accepting her plaque.

"Wow, *thank you*, Mr. Cooper," Winston exclaimed. He raised his award over his head as if it were a trophy.

Jessica shook Chrome Dome's damp hand and slunk off the stage, with Winston scurrying behind her.

Mr. Cooper tapped the microphone. "Attention, please. You're all dismissed. Head straight to your next classes. This is an exciting day for many of you, but keep commotion in the hallways to a minimum."

The students noisily rose from their seats, picked up their papers and book bags, and began filing out of the auditorium.

Jessica saw Winston looking right at her, trying to push toward her through the slow herd of kids. She ducked past two people in front of her to avoid him.

"Hey, Jess, thanks for the morning entertainment," a deep voice said behind her.

She turned around to face Danny Porter, who was wide receiver for the Sweet Valley football team. He smiled at her and pushed his dark hair back from his tanned face.

"Thanks for your *support*," Jessica said. "I heard you hooting back there."

Danny laughed. "It was pretty interesting to watch the geekiest guy in school standing under the spotlight next to the hottest girl."

Jessica rolled her eyes and looked modestly at the floor. She glanced up at him and flashed her prettiest smile. "I wouldn't want anyone to think this whole SAT business meant I was joining the Nerd Club," she said, hoping for another compliment.

"No chance of that." Danny looked her up and down with an appreciative eye. "If I were you, I wouldn't worry too much about being taken for an Egbert-style geek," he whispered in her ear. "Not with your looks."

Jessica felt relieved as she watched Danny disappear into the flow of students moving toward the auditorium doors. Scoring high on the SATs wasn't going to ruin her reputation, after all. It just put her in the center of attention and admiration around school—exactly where she liked to be.

It's just incredible what people really think of me, she pondered. Everyone was probably talking about how cool and fashionable *and* smart she was. Jessica tossed back her silky hair and sashayed out of the auditorium.

Just then John Pfeifer, the *Oracle* sports editor, and Penny Ayala, the school newspaper's editor in chief, walked past Jessica with amused looks on their faces.

"So you scored the big numbers, Jessica," John called out. "It's pretty amazing that even *you* could do something like that."

Jessica stopped walking and the smile wilted from her face. She turned to look at John. "Don't die of shock or anything," she said indignantly.

"Well, people are pretty surprised to find out you're this . . . well . . . that you did so well," Penny said. She shrugged and continued walking down the hall with John.

"Hey, Jess," Jim Roberts said. He was walking by with a camera slung over his shoulder. "How'd you pull it off? Suzanne Hanlon and I were trying to figure out how you had, you know, so much going on."

"I guess I'm just full of surprises," Jessica responded dryly.

"You sure are," David Prentiss agreed, walking by

with Jade Wu. "Jade can't believe you scored so high, either."

"It's just a little unexpected," Jade added politely. "By the way, you look beautiful today, as always. You've always got the greatest outfits on. See you later."

Jessica flashed a brave smile. "Yeah, see you later."

She slumped against her locker, morosely watching people file into classrooms. Jessica felt as if a building had just collapsed on her. Everyone was talking about her, all right. They were telling each other how stunned they were that she actually had a brain.

Elizabeth leaned her forehead against the cool metal of her locker. The award assembly honoring Jessica's high scores was over. Now all she had to do was drag herself to her classes, crawl home, and bury herself in a hole in the backyard.

She yanked open the locker door and lugged out her heavy English and history books. They weighed about a ton more than they had yesterday, before she'd opened her SAT notice. What was the point of even studying anymore? Her scores were so bad, she'd never get into college. She could probably kiss her dream of being a writer good-bye.

"I bet I know what next week's "Personal Profiles" will be about," Olivia Davidson, the arts editor for *The Oracle,* said as she raced by.

"What?" Elizabeth asked lethargically.

"Jessica and her surprise test scores, of

course." Olivia waved and flew into a classroom.

Elizabeth watched Penny Ayala, DeeDee Gordon, and Dana Larson rush through the halls, talking and laughing. She felt like an alien who'd just beamed into the school corridors from Mars and didn't belong there at all.

As Elizabeth glumly wrapped her arms around her books, she saw Todd coming around the corner with Aaron, Barry, and Ron Edwards. When Todd saw her, he motioned excitedly.

Elizabeth felt a current of hope flood through her body, just seeing Todd. She dropped her books onto the floor next to her locker and walked swiftly down the hall, not taking her eyes from his glowing face.

Todd was pulling a letter from an envelope. Elizabeth could see that it was the scholarship-offer notice from the University of Michigan. He showed it to Barry, who read it and let out a whoop.

"We always knew you were a total stud, Wilkins," Barry said, high-fiving Todd.

"Hey, I might still let you breathe the same atmosphere," Todd joked.

"Nice offer," Aaron said. He punched Todd's shoulder. "But I've got to go breathe the atmosphere in Jaworski's history class right now. Catch you later."

Todd waved good-bye to the guys as he replaced the letter in the envelope.

"So what's up with you?" he said, turning his warm gaze to Elizabeth.

She threw her arms around his neck. It felt so

warm and reassuring just to hold him. She pulled back and kissed him lightly on the lips. "Todd, I have to talk to you, I—"

"Liz, the good news is in," Todd interrupted. "I scored in the six hundreds on the SATs—high enough to get the basketball scholarship to Michigan."

Elizabeth dropped her arms to her sides. "That's terrific, Todd," she said, trying to ignore the dull aching in her stomach.

"I'll bet you anything I get other offers," he said cheerfully. He put his hands on her shoulders and looked into her eyes. "Then we can choose."

Elizabeth's knees weakened. "Great."

"So how'd you do on the SATs?"

Elizabeth felt the blood drain from her face. "Not . . . not quite as well as you did," she stammered.

"Well, I got exceptional scores," Todd said with a shrug. "If you got anywhere close, which I'm sure you did, you'll still be in the running for the big leagues with me." He gave her a kiss. "So what did you get?"

"I got—" she began. Suddenly the second bell rang. "I've got to go. I'll tell you later," she whispered.

As Elizabeth picked up her books, hot tears began to roll down her face. There was no way she could confide her scores to Todd now.

With a cold shudder, Elizabeth realized that Todd was going to take off to a top university. And leave her behind.

I'm going to lose him forever, she told herself. *My life is over.*

Chapter 6

Jessica selected a small cucumber-and-tomato salad from the cafeteria lunch line and set her tray down next to Lila and Amy.

"Is that skimpy salad going to be enough to feed that tremendous brain?" Lila asked with a smirk.

"I suppose, like everyone else, you're going into coronary occlusion at the notion that I even *am* smart," Jessica said bitterly. She stabbed a cucumber with her fork.

"Well, maybe not coronary *occlusion*," Amy said, glancing at Lila.

"Ha, ha," Jessica said dryly. "It's nice to know my friends have always had such a high opinion of my basic intelligence."

"Seriously, Jess," Amy said, giving Jessica a light pat on the arm. "Anybody who's ever been on the cheering squad with you knows how fast you think on your feet."

"Thanks, Amy."

Lila stirred her iced tea. "Even those of us who aren't cheerleaders always knew you and Winston were two peas in a pod."

"Right! And it's so nice that you're going to Nerd U together," Amy said enthusiastically as she opened her milk carton.

"Amy and I plan to further ponder how you and Winston were meant for each other this weekend, when she stays overnight," Lila said.

"You mean you're planning to be so bored stiff that Winston and I are all you'll have to talk about?" Jessica said archly.

"Well, we may also discuss going out with the best-looking guys on the SVU volleyball and swim teams." Lila looked at her fingernails. "And how you'll be scavenging for a decent guy at one of those geek colleges back east."

"I see," Jessica responded casually as she jabbed a lettuce leaf.

Jessica spotted the latest issue of her favorite magazine sticking out of Lila's leather shoulder bag. Seeing a picture of a fantastic-looking guy splashed across the cover, Jessica grabbed the magazine.

"This cover story sounds great. 'College Men to Pine For.'" Jessica quickly flipped through the glossy pages until she found the headline article. "Wow, these guys are *gorgeous*," she said with surprise.

"Let me see," Lila said. She tried to take the magazine out of Jessica's hands.

"Not so fast," Jessica said calmly, glancing at Lila with raised eyebrows. "After all, I'll be the one sharing the campus with these hunks. I'll need all the research I can get."

"However, that magazine is my property. And if you think you're going to keep photographs of good-looking men from me—" Lila said, leaning over Jessica.

"The clothes on these guys! They're so suave and sophisticated," Jessica exclaimed. She twisted away so that the magazine was out of Lila's reach. "I love men in long-sleeved polo shirts, don't you?"

"If you don't give me that magazine in one second, I'll—"

"You know, Li, I'm willing to let you have the SVU guys. I think I'll be happy to spend a few years with these incredible male specimens at Yale or Princeton." Jessica looked innocently at Lila. "Mind if I borrow this magazine for a couple of days?"

Lila drummed her long red nails on the table, fuming. Jessica rolled up the magazine and placed it under her arm as she picked up her tray.

"Maybe if Jess spends the night with us at your house this weekend, she'll bring the magazine and share it," Amy said in a loud whisper to Lila.

"All right," Lila said reluctantly. "But no admission without that magazine. I go crazy for prelaw majors in expensive sweaters." Lila's annoyed expression finally gave way to a wry smile.

As Jessica left the table, she felt a flood of relief.

The stupid SATs weren't going to ruin her life, after all, she thought as she patted the magazine under her arm. *This might even be fun. Great-looking, successful guys are always proud to be around smart girls.*

Jessica glided toward the cafeteria door. Just before she stepped out, she caught sight of Ken. His blond hair fell in sexy strands across his forehead, and he looked every inch the star quarterback he was.

Jessica slid into the empty seat next to him and crossed her legs. "See? I was telling you the truth about my scores. Don't you feel lucky having a girlfriend with both looks and brains?" Jessica asked playfully. "It's so crazy, my getting an award for highest SATs." She waited for Ken to beam proudly at her and shower her with adoring praise.

"Right, it's been a pretty weird day," Ken said. He pushed back his chair and picked up his tray. Jessica just stared at him.

"Where are you going?" Jessica asked. "Don't you think it's fun, all this attention I've been getting?"

"Yeah, it's great," Ken said without enthusiasm.

She stood up and lightly touched his cheek, but he refused to look directly at her. Jessica felt a stab in her heart as she remembered last night at Cafe Feliz. Ken had been so annoyingly understanding when he'd believed she'd got low scores.

"I have to get to class," he said quickly.

"Your next class doesn't start for twenty minutes," she objected. "Look at me," she said, placing a hand on his forearm. He finally met her gaze, but she couldn't quite read the emotion she saw in his deep-blue eyes.

"I'm sorry, I really have to go, Jess. I'll call you," Ken said quietly.

Jessica's eyes stung with tears. Why was her boyfriend acting like a stranger?

Elizabeth turned off her desk light and stared into the darkness. She was supposed to be reading a play for Mr. Collins's English class, but in the last twenty minutes she'd read the same line over and over about fifty times. She threw the play aside, defeated.

A dark lump of college applications caught her eye, from where they were gathering dust in the corner of her room. She wouldn't have to apply to colleges until the middle of senior year, but she'd asked a number of them to send their forms early, so she could look them over.

With a sigh, she flicked on the desk lamp again and picked up one of the applications. "Describe your long-term goals." Elizabeth set her pen point at the top of the page. She wrote a sentence and crossed it out. She wrote another and scratched a heavy line through it. Finally, she flung the pen against her Shakespeare poster and crumpled the application into a ball.

She stared at the notebook page scrawled with her half-finished "Personal Profiles" column about Jessica. She was supposed to turn it in to Mr. Collins tomorrow morning. *Why can't I just make myself finish it?*

she wondered. *Maybe because I feel like a fraud even being on the newspaper staff!*

Elizabeth stood up, then threw herself facedown onto the bed. Brushing angry tears from her cheeks, she reached for a paperback book from her small bedside shelf and opened to the first page. All she wanted to do was get absorbed in a good murder mystery and not think about the future.

She read three pages and threw down the book in disgust. Reading had always lifted her spirits, but now it seemed as pointless as everything else. Maybe she shouldn't even be reading books—maybe she should be in the garage, learning to weld. She was so frustrated, she thought she'd explode. It was so unfair!

Jessica stuck her head in the door. "Lizzie, can I borrow your college catalogs?"

"I thought you wanted to go to a party school," Elizabeth snapped.

"Well, I guess I changed my mind," Jessica said, placing her hands on her hips. "Just let me look at your books."

Elizabeth sprang from the bed, picked up a load of catalogs, and threw them at Jessica. "Here, you can keep them, since I'm obviously headed for vocational school."

"Hey, what's your problem?" Jessica ducked the flying catalogs. "Is it *my* fault you got lousy scores?"

"No, of course it's not your fault, Jess," Elizabeth said quietly. Exhausted, she fell back onto her bed. "I just have to face up to the fact that I'm not the person everyone's always thought I was."

"Cheer up, Liz. You can always come visit me at college. I'll probably be buddies with the captain of the men's lacrosse team or something, and he'll have a good-looking roommate," Jessica said, gathering up the catalogs and walking to the door.

"What an offer!" Elizabeth yelled as Jessica slammed the door.

Elizabeth sank her head into her pillow and stared at the ceiling. She pictured herself taking the weekend off from her job as a forklift operator to visit Jessica at some fancy college. Great. She slammed her fist into the mattress. *I should have scored as high as Jessica. What went wrong?*

Jessica dumped Elizabeth's college catalogs onto her bed, then shoved together a pile of clothes. She sat comfortably on top of a small hill of rumpled T-shirts.

She opened one of the catalogs, in search of cute guys. One photograph showed a Yale man standing on a hill in a cabled sweater and corduroy pants, with a book under his arm and the wind blowing through his dark hair. He was even better looking than the guys in Lila's magazine.

Jessica imagined herself in a cozy ski lodge in Vermont, nestled by the fire with this handsome Ivy Leaguer. Or hiking to a secluded spot in the Catskills with a rugged Harvard guy. Exhausted from the long, arduous climb, they would sink into the Alpine grass and melt into a passionate kiss.

She could see herself sitting in a crowded nightclub

in New York City, holding hands with a sophisticated artist from Columbia University. He would look magnetically into her crystal-blue eyes and tell her he was allured by her slender body, but fascinated by the mysterious workings of her mind.

Jessica opened a fresh catalog and looked slowly through the student pictures. These guys were definitely gorgeous enough to be her type. Maybe being a brain wasn't so bad, after all.

In the margins next to the action shots of the college men were blurbs about their achievements. Each of the guys, with his muscular body and fashionably cut hair, was studying a subject like chemistry, history, art, physics.

These guys are all going someplace, she thought.

Jessica had never buckled down to anything in her life. She loved partying, shopping, and cheerleading. But was she hiding whole pieces of her personality behind clothes and charm? Was it possible that Jessica could get attention from great guys *and* study art or science—all at the same time?

Elizabeth dropped her completed "Personal Profiles" column into the in box on Mr. Collins's desk and turned away.

Mr. Collins looked up and smiled. "Great, I was just wondering when you were going to brighten my day with another excellent article. Can't wait to look at it."

"I don't know how good it is," Elizabeth said in a

small voice. "But I knew you needed it this morning." She shrugged apologetically.

He gazed at her with slightly narrowed eyes. "What's up, Liz?" Mr. Collins asked, jotting notes on an article. "You seem a little down. Why don't you have a seat?"

Elizabeth lowered herself into the chair across from his desk, her heart pounding. "Mr. Collins, I made a decision this morning. I might as well tell you and get it over with."

"What decision?" He put down his pen and gave her his full attention.

Elizabeth steeled herself. "I'm resigning from *The Oracle*," she said, hearing the tremor in her voice. She'd promised herself she wouldn't cry, but as soon as she spoke, she felt tears rise in her throat. Elizabeth wanted to run into the hills above Sweet Valley and hide forever.

"Now, slow down just a second and tell me what's happened," Mr. Collins said, watching her.

Elizabeth took a deep breath. She often came to Mr. Collins to talk over problems or ask for advice, but she'd rather die than let anyone find out about her SAT scores. What if he laughed at her and actually agreed that she was better off quitting *The Oracle*?

Elizabeth opened her mouth to speak. Before she could get a word out, two tears slid down her cheeks. Mr. Collins pulled a tissue out of a box on his desk and handed it to her.

"Mr. Collins, I got my SAT scores back and

they're awful," Elizabeth cried, soaking up fresh tears with the tissue. "I'll never get into college now, and I'll never be a writer."

She buried her face in her hands so she wouldn't have to see his reaction. He probably realized now that she was actually a terrible English student. Her stomach froze into a solid chunk of ice.

"Elizabeth, the SATs are just one set of tests. The scores people get are influenced by lots of factors," she heard him say.

She lifted her head and looked directly into Mr. Collins's face. "They are?"

"Sure," he responded confidently. "Elizabeth, you're the best writer I've seen in twelve years of teaching English and advising on *The Oracle*. One bad run on a standardized test doesn't take that away from you."

She studied his serious expression and saw that he wasn't making fun of her.

"Really?" she asked, barely audibly.

"Really," he answered.

"But aren't the SATs important?" Elizabeth insisted. "Don't they prove something about how smart you are—or aren't?"

"They're one measurement of intelligence," Mr. Collins said thoughtfully, folding his hands on his stomach. "But first of all, these exams test for quick reaction time on pattern recognition, not creativity," he explained. "And second of all, many people who are very intelligent and very good at discerning patterns—like you—don't do well on the SATs."

"Why wouldn't they do well?" Elizabeth asked, shifting anxiously in her seat and hanging on to every word Mr. Collins said.

He picked up his pen and tapped it on the table. "Well, it might be as simple as not getting enough sleep the night before."

"Or maybe they worry so much about the test that when they finally do take it, they're too nervous to concentrate?" Elizabeth asked.

"Maybe," Mr. Collins said. "Or they could be more comfortable taking their time than with filling in blanks under pressure."

"But I always thought I was good under time pressure. At least, I know I'm good at meeting newspaper deadlines. Have I been wrong?" Elizabeth drooped miserably in her chair.

"What do you think?" Mr. Collins asked warmly, his eyes crinkling at the corners. "Elizabeth, listen carefully to me—I want to tell you something important."

"Yes?" Elizabeth said weakly.

Mr. Collins leaned forward in his chair. "No test is capable of measuring the depth of your intelligence and insight," he said sincerely. "If you want badly enough to be a writer, and you keep working as hard as you always have in my class and on my newspaper staff, then you'll be a writer."

"Do you honestly believe that?" Elizabeth said doubtfully.

"Yes, I honestly believe it. Speaking of which, you can't walk off my staff now. I need you," he declared.

"In fact, I'd like to give you a special assignment. Write an essay on anything you'd like for next week's *Oracle.*"

Elizabeth felt herself relax a little. But a fresh wave of depair swept over her as another detail of crushing reality became apparent.

"I appreciate your trying to encourage me, Mr. Collins. But I'll never get accepted into college. Even if I'm a good writer, I still have horrible test scores."

"That may hinder you some, but not as much as you think," Mr. Collins answered. "Where did you get the idea that a bad day in the exam room will automatically bar you from a good college?"

"I don't understand," Elizabeth said, puzzled.

"Liz, admissions departments will look at everything in your record. They'll see that you have consistently high grades, great teacher recommendations, leadership skills, extracurricular activities—not to mention the undying admiration of your school's newpaper adviser," he said.

"Thanks, Mr. Collins," Elizabeth said, looking down.

He smiled. "Don't thank me. It's all the result of your hard work," he said. "You can also have personal interviews with representatives from the colleges, and they'll realize what a fine addition you'll make to their academic community."

Elizabeth stood up. "I feel better just talking it over, instead of keeping it all bottled up inside."

Mr. Collins straightened up a few papers on his desk. "When you can talk honestly about your concerns with friends, things don't seem quite so bad."

"I guess you're right."

"And speaking of the SATs," Mr. Collins added, with a sideways look. "Jessica's success on the exams is certainly unexpected. She was never much of a worker in my class, but I'm aware of the fact that she's a very bright girl."

"My sister's smart when she wants to be," Elizabeth agreed.

She walked out of the room, wishing she could feel happy for her sister. Shaking her head, she realized it would be easier if she believed Mr. Collins's assurances that there was hope for her own future.

Chapter 7

"I've never seen you do such careful lab work," Dan Scott said. Jessica was measuring out vials of chemicals in Mr. Harrison's Wednesday-morning chemistry class.

"Want to come over to my house later and perform some experiments?" Winston clowned from the other lab bench. Jessica glared at him.

"Well," she said, turning her attention to Dan, "I figure that since I'm a top SAT scorer, I might as well complete one lab assignment."

Dan nodded with approval. "That's the spirit."

Jessica had been daydreaming since class started about being partnered in a college chem lab with an extremely handsome fellow student. Someone like Dan would do fine.

Jessica held her test tube of liquid up to the light. Yes, she was definitely getting used to the idea of her

SAT scores rocketing her into the collegiate company of the smartest, best-looking guys in the country.

The lab door creaked open, and Rosemary, Chrome Dome's secretary, looked in and glanced around, resting her gaze on Jessica.

"Jessica, Mr. Cooper would like to see you in his office right away. He says it's rather urgent."

"He probably wants to congratulate you in a less zoolike setting than an all-school assembly," Maria said, squinting into her microscope.

"Dan, could you baby-sit my test tubes for a few minutes?" Jessica asked, batting her eyelashes. "I wouldn't want to waste a perfectly good experiment."

He smiled sweetly. "Sure, I understand."

Jessica grinned flirtatiously and waltzed out of the lab.

Mr. Cooper was standing at the window of his office, his hands clasped behind his back.

"Hi, Mr. Cooper," Jessica said cheerfully as she sailed into the room and shut the door.

He turned and stared grimly at her, then sat behind his desk and adjusted his glasses on his prominent nose. "Please sit down, Ms. Wakefield."

"My friends all call me Jessica," she chirped as she flopped into the wooden chair across from him.

He peered expressionlessly over his glasses. Chrome Dome wasn't known for his sparkling sense of humor. Still, this wasn't the greeting Jessica expected from someone who had lavished praise on her

71

twenty-four hours earlier. She shifted uncomfortably in the hard chair and cleared her throat.

"Is something wrong?" Jessica asked.

"Wrong, yes," Chrome Dome mumbled. "Something is very wrong. It seems that some serious charges are being made." He took off his glasses and polished them on his shirt.

"Charges?" Jessica repeated, confused.

Chrome Dome replaced the glasses. "I'm afraid, young lady, that the school board believes there's strong evidence that you cheated on the SATs."

Jessica blinked. "Excuse me, Mr. Cooper. I don't mean to be rude, but what are you talking about?"

"The board reviews records for each class for the purpose of collecting statistics about the Sweet Valley school system," he explained. "They match grades, attitude, and previous testing performance against SAT scores."

"So?"

"Well, frankly, Miss Wakefield, looking at the whole picture, I must say your stellar achievement does look suspicious."

Jessica clenched her hands into fists in her lap. The accusation was insane, and she refused even to dignify it with a denial.

"I'm sorry they feel that way," she said in a low, controlled voice. Jessica stood up and took a step toward the door.

"So," Chrome Dome continued, "in order to reinstate your scores, it will be necessary for you to re-take the SATs."

Jessica froze with her hand on the brass door-knob. She turned slowly and stared at Chrome Dome, feeling hot anger boiling up in her.

"Retake the—" Jessica began incredulously. She took a deep breath and gathered her composure. "Look, I may not be your model student, but I got those scores fair and square. I refuse on principle to retake that test."

Mr. Cooper rose to his feet and pressed both palms on the desk. "I'm afraid it's not that simple, Jessica. If you resist cooperating, you'll be making serious trouble for yourself."

"Well, you can have my award plaque back, if that's what you want," Jessica said, seething.

Chrome Dome's face turned red, with veins standing out on his neck and temples. "You could risk suspension for the remainder of the year—you may not be able to graduate with your class."

Jessica felt as if she'd been kicked in the stomach. She'd been in trouble before, but always for minor things. Her punishment usually amounted to an hour of detention.

But not graduating with her class! She'd be the laughingstock of the school, and she hadn't even done anything wrong. This was a certifiable outrage.

"Do you have anything to say, Jessica?" Chrome Dome asked impatiently.

"Just this," she replied, trembling with rage. "You

and the school board do whatever you have to do. But I'm not retaking that test. Do you know why?"

"Because you're foolish and obstinate," Chrome Dome said, his voice rising.

"No," Jessica said quietly. "Because I'm innocent." She pulled open the door and walked out.

Elizabeth sat down across from Todd at their favorite table in the school cafeteria. She poured dressing over her chef's salad.

Her stomach was full of butterflies, but she knew she had to share the truth with Todd. He always listened to her when she really needed him.

"Todd, I need to talk to you about my SAT scores," Elizabeth said in a calm, direct voice.

Todd took a bite out of his turkey sandwich. He was absorbed in a letter he'd smoothed out on the table in front of him.

"Todd? Did you hear what I said?" Elizabeth asked.

"Huh? Liz, you won't believe this. I got four more scholarship offers in the mail yesterday. The University of Pennsylvania is sending their basketball coach to watch me play in the big game next month."

"That's great, Todd. You really deserve it. But, listen, I have to tell you some—"

"I mean, do you realize I'm going to be up for scholarships at not only Michigan and U Penn, but also Yale, Harvard, and Princeton?" Todd went on.

"That's totally awesome," Elizabeth said emphatically. "But I need your support, too, Todd. I didn't do well on the SATs." She paused. "In fact, my scores were pretty low," she continued, summoning all the courage she could muster.

"Low? How low?" Todd said distractedly. He held his sandwich in one hand and the letter in the other.

"I scored four-ninety in English and four-eighty in Math," she answered, closing her eyes momentarily. She prayed for him to give her a hug and tell her he still loved her and was still proud of her.

When she opened her eyes, Todd had stopped chewing and was staring at her.

"Mr. Collins says it's not as bad as it might look on the surface," she babbled nervously. "He says colleges look at lots of criteria, and bad scores don't mean I'm stupid, and, uh—"

"You know, Liz, those scores aren't so terrible. I mean, that's probably above the national average. You can go to lots of schools," Todd said. He set the letter down.

"But, Todd, I want to go to one of the best universities in the country. My scores don't come anywhere near qualifying me for the Ivy Leagues."

Todd shrugged. "Well, it looks like you might have to rethink your goals for the future," he said. "But I'm sure everything will work out in the long run."

Elizabeth felt as if the ground were sliding out from beneath her. "Todd, I need your support," she said, trying not to sound desperate. "How could this have happened after I studied so hard? You don't think I'm stupid, do you?"

Elizabeth stopped breathing and touched Todd's hand. He caressed her fingers, then gently pulled his hand away.

"Todd, you still believe in me, don't you?" Elizabeth whispered. She looked at him with pleading, glistening eyes.

"It's a tough break, Liz. But I'm sure you'll be OK." He shrugged and picked up his letter again.

Elizabeth felt as if the slipping ground beneath her had become a full-blown mud slide.

Todd shook his head and chuckled. "Five major universities fighting over me." He was obviously talking to himself and hardly even knew she was there anymore. "It's too cool for words. I never thought this would happen to me."

"Todd," Elizabeth said hoarsely, giving it one more try, "do you think the admissions departments at those universities might overlook my scores and take my entire record—my entire life—into account?" Just one word of encouragement from Todd would help her find the strength she needed to pick herself up from this defeat.

"I don't know, Liz. I honestly don't know what to tell you." He stood up. "I've got an appointment in ten minutes to talk to the college adviser about my options. See you later." He gave her a quick kiss on the cheek and walked away.

Elizabeth carefully lifted her napkin to her face so

76

that no one in the cafeteria could see her cry. She dried the few tears that sprang to her eyes, then crumpled the napkin into her fist. She and Todd were supposed to be planning their futures together, but he hadn't even been listening to her.

Todd's full of his own future, Elizabeth thought, tearing the napkin into shreds. *But he doesn't seem to care at all about mine.*

"Hey, give that napkin a break," Enid said, setting her lunch tray down next to Elizabeth.

"Oh, hi, Enid," Elizabeth sighed. She released the napkin confetti onto the table. "I guess I was getting a little flustered with Todd. He's suddenly become big man on campus."

Enid rolled her eyes. "Tell me about it," she said. "Forget him for a minute. I've got some news for you." She spooned some yogurt into her mouth.

"Don't say the word 'news.'" Elizabeth stared without interest at her chef's salad. "It makes me think of *The Oracle,* and that makes me think of an editorial I'm not sure I have the enthusiasm to write."

"Well, worry about that later," Enid advised, digging into a fruit salad. "Chrome Dome hauled Jessica into his office this morning. The school board thinks she cheated on the SATs."

Elizabeth lifted her glazed stare from her wilting salad to her best friend's face.

"Cheated?" she said.

"You heard me. And rumors are flying that she

erased the name on your test and wrote in hers instead—and wrote your name on her exam," Enid said.

"What?" Elizabeth gasped, her eyes wide.

Enid shrugged. "That's what people are saying."

"But how . . . how . . . could that have happened?" Elizabeth stuttered. She felt as if she were underwater, straining to understand what she was hearing. "Are you sure?"

"Yeah, pretty sure. I mean, word's traveled fast," Enid replied.

"But Jessica left the exam early and went home." Elizabeth's heart was hammering wildly.

"Caroline Pearce swears she saw Jessica step back into the classroom after everyone else left."

"Caroline Pearce is an incorrigible gossip," Elizabeth said. She stuck a carrot stick into her mouth.

"Terri said the same thing. She heard it from Shelley. And Tony was almost positive he saw Jessica hanging around the halls after she supposedly finished her test."

Elizabeth speared a slice of boiled egg. She felt blood pounding in her ears.

"Besides," Enid continued, "we're talking about Jessica. How could she have finished that fast and done that well? Unless—"

"Unless," Elizabeth whispered hoarsely.

"Unless she cheated," Enid said. She bit into a peach.

Elizabeth drove the fork into the center of her salad. Jessica's attitude toward the SATs had been so strangely casual, while everyone else had been studying their guts out. And then there were Jessica's cryptic remarks about how her life would turn out fine—one way or another. Elizabeth even thought of the dishes and kitchen mess her sister always left lying around; she consistently demonstrated total lack of concern for anyone but herself.

Jessica couldn't care less about planning for the future—and she was apparently willing to drag Elizabeth down with her.

I knew something had gone wrong with that test, and now it all adds up, she thought with growing conviction.

"This is the last straw," Elizabeth murmured, shoving back her chair and jumping angrily to her feet.

"What are you doing? What's going on?" Enid asked, concerned.

"Just a little family business to take care of," Elizabeth said through clenched teeth.

Enid looked bewildered. "What about your salad?"

"Feed it to the rats. There are plenty of them crawling around in this school."

Jessica's hand shook as she reached for a bowl of fruit salad in the school lunch line. Her whole body was still trembling from her insulting meeting with Chrome Dome.

People had seen her storm out of his office; they were already spreading rumors about what they claimed to have heard. Jessica realized it was critical to get her version of what had happened around school fast.

She pressed a cool glass of ice tea against her scalding face and spotted Caroline Pearce. Jessica's eyes lit up. Caroline was a notorious school gossip; Jessica didn't like Caroline much, but she was the fastest telegraph service available.

"Hi, Caroline," Jessica sang sweetly.

"Oh, hi, Jess," Caroline said, her eyes wide. "We were just talking about you a minute ago." Caroline shot a knowing glance at Amanda Hayes, who was sitting across the table from her.

"You were?" Jessia asked innocently. *I bet. You look like a barracuda who's just spied some fat prey.* "Caroline, I've been dying to talk to you. You won't believe what happened." Jessica leaned forward confidentially.

Caroline froze with her cupcake halfway to her mouth. "What?"

"Well, Mr. Cooper says the school board thinks I cheated on the SATs," Jessica whispered into Caroline's ear.

"No!" Caroline said, looking quickly at Amanda.

"Yes! Isn't that ridiculous? It's a totally unjust accusation," Jessica said, enunciating every word. "And not only that, Chrome Dome tried to intimidate me into confessing."

"He did?"

"Yeah, but I stood my ground. I'm not guilty."

"Does anyone else know about this?" Caroline

asked. She was obviously champing at the bit to spread the juicy news.

"No. And please don't tell anyone," Jessica said solemnly.

"Your secret's safe with me," Caroline said. She looked frantically around the room, then scrambled to her feet and grabbed her tray.

"Thanks, Caroline," Jessica said with a grateful smile. "I knew I could count on you."

"Uh, I've got to go. I need to talk to Suzanne about . . . something . . . before she leaves the lunchroom. 'Bye." Caroline raced across the room.

Jessica dropped her smile and arched an eyebrow as she watched Caroline scuttle over to Suzanne's table.

The story of that stupid accusation and my total innocence will be all over school in about three minutes, she thought. Jessica relaxed and savored a cool chunk of pineapple. This whole business about her cheating would be diffused before it could get out of hand.

"I need a word with you," said a tight, icy voice.

Jessica looked up and saw Elizabeth glaring down at her, purple-faced and stiff as a board.

"What's the matter?" Jessica asked. She spooned up a strawberry.

"I'll tell you what's the matter," Elizabeth exploded. "You cheated on the SATs! You stole my exam scores by writing my name on your test!"

"Are you out of your mind?" Jessica said, dropping her jaw. It was crazy enough that she'd been accused of cheating in the first place. *But stealing Elizabeth's scores?*

Elizabeth's eyes were blazing. "You've always been jealous of me, you always want to do things the easy way, and you never think about anyone else's feelings," she accused.

"Well, that just goes to show how little you know me," Jessica yelled.

People all over the cafeteria stopped their conversations and stared in total shock.

Jessica slammed her bowl down on the table and stood up, her nose inches from Elizabeth's. "And if my exceptional understanding of history serves me, in this country people are innocent until proven guilty. If you were a little *smarter,* maybe you'd understand that."

Elizabeth's face crumpled, as if she'd been struck. She narrowed her eyes.

"I'm smart enough to know that you walked all over my hard work to get what you want. You know perfectly well that no one believes you could really have gotten those scores, Jessica."

Jessica recoiled and her hands balled into fists. This was it. She'd had enough.

"So it's true!" Jessica screamed. "Everyone, including my own sister, thinks I'm stupid. Well, you're going to discover otherwise when the truth finally comes out!"

Jessica glared at her sister, then turned on her heel and stalked out of the cafeteria.

Chapter 8

Elizabeth stormed into the house on Wednesday afternoon. She set her books down on the hall table, then glowered as Jessica came in after her, slamming the door.

"I feel confident that we can finish the design job for you within two weeks," Alice Wakefield said into the hall telephone. She wrote a note on the message pad and glanced at the two girls.

Elizabeth gave her mother the best excuse for a smile she could come up with, given the fact that she still wanted to wring Jessica's neck. Fuming, Elizabeth brushed past Jessica and hung her jacket on a wooden peg. Jessica threw her windbreaker onto a chair and made a show of keeping her head turned away from Elizabeth. They hadn't spoken a word to each other during the entire tense drive home, which suited Elizabeth just fine.

"Then I'll talk to you next week," Mrs. Wakefield said into the phone, eyeing first Elizabeth and then Jessica, with one eyebrow raised. "All right, good-bye." She set down the phone and looked questioningly at each of them.

Elizabeth strode into the kitchen with her chin jutted out. Jessica followed.

"Is there something going on that I should know about?" Mrs. Wakefield called from the hallway.

Elizabeth glanced at Jessica. "Planning to tell Mom you've been accused of cheating?" she whispered testily.

"Actually, I thought I'd make casual conversation about your paranoid jealousy," Jessica replied.

"Girls?"

Elizabeth looked narrowly at her sister. "Nothing, Mom, just a long day at school!" she called.

"You can say that again," Jessica mumbled fiercely under her breath. She swung open the refrigerator and rummaged aggressively through the contents.

"Oh, shut up," Elizabeth hissed between clenched teeth. She ripped open a box of crackers.

"What?" her mother called again from the hallway.

"We're fine, Mom!" Jessica shouted. She dumped three tablespoonfuls of cottage cheese into a bowl and stared hatefully at Elizabeth.

Then she picked up her bowl and started striding out of the kitchen. "Excuse me, you're blocking the doorway," she said curtly.

"Pardon me, Your Majesty," Elizabeth responded.

Jessica stepped past Elizabeth, who marched into the living room after her. Elizabeth collapsed into her favorite armchair and stuffed cheese and crackers into her mouth.

Jessica hauled a huge book off one of the book-shelves. Then she flopped onto the couch and started conspicuously reading *War and Peace*.

"That's a pretty thick book," Elizabeth observed. "Rather uncharacteristic of you, isn't it?"

"Quiet, I'm reading," Jessica barked, her nose buried in the text.

"Why don't you just read it in the original Russian, instead of bothering with the watered-down English version?" Elizabeth asked sarcastically.

"Maybe I'll do just that," Jessica snapped. "I should be able to pick up the language in a semester or two when I get to a first-rate East Coast college."

Elizabeth snorted. "Ha, you'll flunk out in the first semester." She picked up a notebook and pen from the floor by the chair and began writing furiously.

"You need to take your crystal ball in for repairs—it's not doing you much good these days," Jessica shot back. "And could you try not annoying me with trivial conversation? It disturbs my concentration." Jessica bit furiously into an apple.

"I've got the start of a good history paper here," Elizabeth announced. "I think I'll read it aloud, just to hear how it sounds so far." Elizabeth cleared her throat. "The twentieth century has seen a marked decline in ethics, compared with the previous two centuries in American history—"

"Oh, spare me," Jessica interrupted.

"Ambition has overtaken integrity in every corner of the culture—"

"I swear, I'm going to gag if you don't shut up."

"Lying, theft, and betrayal have become commonplace. Even among close friends and family we see—"

The telephone on the hall table rang. Both Elizabeth and Jessica jumped up to grab the receiver. They stopped when they heard Mrs. Wakefield's voice. "Oh, hello, Mr. Cooper," she said cheerfully.

Elizabeth saw Jessica grip the door frame.

"Yes, I have a moment," Mrs. Wakefield said, her forehead slightly creased. She picked up a ballpoint pen and poised it over the message pad. But instead of writing, she began nervously clicking the pen top with her thumb.

After a few moments her face went slack. Mrs. Wakefield gently replaced the phone on its hook. She bent over, picked up the pen, and quietly tapped it on her palm.

"We'll talk about this later, Jessica," she said calmly. Then she turned and left the room.

Elizabeth gazed at Jessica. She had no idea what her parents would say, but she knew Jessica could be in hot water.

"Hey, Jess?"

Jessica slowly turned her head toward Elizabeth. Her face was as white as a sheet, but the expression on it was proud and angry. Elizabeth searched her sister's features for signs of guilt, but saw none.

"Would you pass the salad, Alice?" Ned Wakefield asked. Jessica noted that those were the first words anyone had spoken in about ten minutes.

Mrs. Wakefield passed the wooden salad bowl to Elizabeth, who passed it to Mr. Wakefield.

"Here you go."

"Thanks."

They all fell back to eating, the clink of silverware punctuating the uncomfortable silence. Jessica couldn't stand to wait anymore for her parents to bring up Chrome Dome and his accusations.

"I need to call Maria about the cheerleading-practice schedule for the week," Jessica said. She pushed her chair back and stood up quickly.

Mr. Wakefield glanced at Mrs. Wakefield.

"Not so fast, Jess, sit back down. We need to talk about Mr. Cooper's call," Mrs. Wakefield said.

Jessica remained standing.

"I didn't do it. He's wrong. They're all wrong," she blurted out. She clutched her fingers around the top of the chair until her knuckles turned white.

Mr. Wakefield set down his fork. "We're not accusing you of anything. Settle down."

Jessica leaned both elbows on the table. "So what did he say?"

"Well, he told us what I think he told you," her mother said. She carefully pushed back her chair. "If

87

you refuse to take the test again, the school board will ask for your suspension."

"Which means you might not graduate with your class," Mr. Wakefield said.

Jessica felt every cell in her body contract. "You *are* accusing me of cheating. You're against me, too. Admit it, you don't think I'm smart enough to have got those scores on my own," she wailed, tears of rage spilling onto her cheeks.

"Jessica, we don't believe for a second that you cheated," Mr. Wakefield said, rubbing his chin thoughtfully. "And of course we know you're smart enough to achieve high SAT scores."

"That's why we get after you about your schoolwork," Mrs. Wakefield added. "Because we know how much potential you have."

Jessica slid back in her chair. "You want me to turn into a nerd, like Elizabeth?" Elizabeth kicked her lightly under the table.

"We want you to be yourself," Mr. Wakefield replied patiently.

"Which means being able to stay in school with your peer group and develop in your own way," her mother said. "That's why it's necessary to retake the test."

Jessica's stomach twisted into knots. "But I got those scores without cheating. You just said you believe me," she pleaded.

"We do believe you," Mr. Wakefield said sincerely. "But the school board has set the rules according to their criteria. Just to clear up the matter, we expect you to take the test again."

"It's not a suggestion. It's a command." Mrs. Wakefield poured water into her glass.

Jessica pounded her fist on the table, rattling the dishes. "This is an outrage!" she yelled. "I won't do it. It's not fair." She rose from the table and began to stalk toward the living room.

"That's too bad," Mr. Wakefield continued. "Because after you'd taken the exam again, I was planning to let you girls take a few days off from school to visit Steven at SVU," he said. "I was even going to throw in some spending money."

Jessica wheeled around and faced her family. Missing school? Partying college-style? Money to go out to discos and nightclubs? Visiting their brother, Steven, who was a freshman at SVU would be a blast, and Lila would be positively green with envy.

"Is this a real offer?" Jessica asked, casting her father a sideways glance.

"Only if you retake the test—just as a formality," Mr. Wakefield answered.

"Fine," Jessica announced. She defiantly placed her hands on her hips. "I'll retake the stupid test."

She would ace the SATs again. That would show everyone once and for all the injustice of the accusation against her.

Elizabeth sat at her desk after dinner and added another sentence to her history paper on declining ethics. "In the modern world, we are quick to accuse the innocent of crimes they haven't committed."

She set down her pen and stared out the window at the starry night, thinking about the accusation against Jessica. Maybe Jessica really was innocent. After all, stealing exam scores wasn't exactly in character for her. *If anyone knows how little my sister cares about tests, it's me,* Elizabeth thought with a sigh.

But if Jessica didn't cheat, then that meant Elizabeth really did do horribly on the SATs. Everyone on the planet knew Jessica's scores by now, but Elizabeth's blood froze at the thought of what everyone would say when they found out *her* scores. The simple truth was that she wasn't as smart as everyone had always thought.

She stood up, walked to her bookshelves, and took out the notebooks of poetry she'd written over the years. Laying them out on the floor, along with the folders of her best English and history essays, she began reading the papers, one by one. Elizabeth felt as if someone else had written them, and fought down a sudden impulse to bundle up her years of writing and burn it all.

"Looks like it's snowing English assignments in here," said a kind, deep voice.

Mr. Wakefield had appeared in the doorway. He leaned against the frame with his hands in his pockets, surveying the cluttered floor.

"Hi, Dad," Elizabeth said, glancing up. "Just looking at some old stuff."

"Oh? And what makes you so nostalgic about your writing tonight?" her father asked.

"I don't know," she said with a shrug.

"Sounds like things are a little heated up at school," he said. He stepped over the papers and sat down on the edge of Elizabeth's bed. "Boy, I remember taking the SATs. Emotions can run pretty high. By the way, Liz, you still haven't told us exactly what your scores were."

"I . . . I don't want to talk about it, Dad," Elizabeth answered. She began putting her papers away and setting the folders back on the shelf, avoiding her father's gaze.

"Just in case they're not as high as you would have liked—or not as high as Jessica's—it's not the end of the world. I promise," Mr. Wakefield said.

Eliabeth gripped the edge of the wooden shelves and turned toward her father. "But I didn't even break five hundred on either section. Does it mean I'm stupid?"

"Elizabeth, of course you're not stupid. That's the craziest notion I've ever heard," Mr. Wakefield said gently. "You're extremely bright, and we're very proud of you, with or without the SATs."

"You are?" she asked, tears welling up in her eyes.

Mr. Wakefield looked thoughtfully at Elizabeth. "Liz, Jessica is going to retake the exam. Why don't you do the same?"

The prospect of taking the test again didn't exactly thrill her. Wasn't one humiliation enough?

"What if I don't do better the second time?" Elizabeth said, staring straight ahead at her bookshelf.

"But what if you do much better the second time?" Mr. Wakefield asked. "How will you know what you can do if you don't risk trying?"

"OK," Elizabeth said, bowing her head with a sigh of resignation. "I'll do it."

"I'm glad you called tonight," Jessica said to Ken. "I really needed to get out of the house."

Jessica squeezed Ken's arm as they approached the double doors of the Dairi Burger. He'd been so strange to her in the cafeteria yesterday, but his voice over the phone tonight had been warm and soothing, sending electric currents through her entire body. He'd obviously forgotten about whatever had been bothering him.

As they headed for their usual booth, Jessica noticed that all conversation seemed to stop. But she held her head high and ignored the rude stares.

Ken sat down in the booth, and Jessica slid in next to him, hearing the whispered sound of her name coming from other tables. She snapped open a menu. "I could go for a strawberry sundae."

Jessica glanced up and noticed Caroline narrowly eyeing her from a nearby table, where she was sitting with two other girls. Jessica gave her a big smile.

"Totally unjust accusation?" Caroline sneered. "That's not what *I* heard." She raised her nose in the air and turned back to her friends.

"Are you sure you want to be here?" Ken asked Jessica in a low voice.

"You bet," Jessica said, intensely examining the menu's choice of sundae toppings. "I'm not going to be run out of my favorite hangout spot by some two-faced gossip and her snide comments."

"Sometimes I'm not sure if you're brave or crazy." Ken touched her lightly under the chin, then signaled for the waitress.

Jessica peered over the top of her menu and noticed her least-favorite person in Sweet Valley, Heather Mallone, staring at her from another table. She was surrounded by a group of cheerleaders, including Amy, Sandy Bacon, and Annie Whitman. Heather slowly pushed herself up from the table, hooked her thumbs in her skintight jeans, and strolled toward Ken and Jessica.

"Don't look now, but the Bride of Dracula is approaching our table," Jessica said under her breath. "No wonder she has to suck blood. Those jeans must totally cut off her circulation."

Heather sauntered up and leaned casually on Ken and Jessica's table with one hand. "How are you tonight, Jessica?" Heather asked.

"I was fine until approximately three seconds ago." Jessica peeled the paper off a straw. "By the way, don't lean on the table. It might break under your weight."

"I don't think so, I'm not the one who just ordered a strawberry sundae loaded with walnuts and M&M's," Heather said coolly.

"I guess some of us are just lucky. We can stay thin without being pathologically obsessed about our weight all the time," Jessica came back smoothly.

"Listen, I'd love to chat with you about diets, but we actually have a little business to discuss." Heather's voice was like silk. Jessica wanted to strangle her.

"Get to the point."

"All right," Heather drawled. "I understand you cheated on the SATs."

"You understand nothing," Jessica shot back, glaring at Heather. Ever since Heather had come to Sweet Valley and wormed her way into being Jessica's cocaptain on the cheerleading squad, she'd been the bane of Jessica's existence.

Heather glanced at her nails. "Well, the squad thinks you should resign—just until this whole thing blows over, of course. It's bad for school spirit to have you stay on."

"I've got news for you," Jessica said, stepping out of the booth. "Being one of the squad leaders doesn't make you the last word, Heather. Excuse me, Ken, I'm going over to talk to Amy and Sandy."

Jessica stormed toward the table of cheerleaders.

"I wouldn't do that if I were you," Heather called after her.

"What's this stuff about knocking me off the squad for something I didn't do?" Jessica demanded, pulling up a seat next to Amy.

Sandy took a sip of her soda and Amy coughed,

tucking her hair behind her ears. No one spoke or looked directly at Jessica.

"Amy?" Jessica asked, puzzled.

"I'm sorry, Jess," Amy finally answered. "It's what's best for the squad—for now."

"What do you mean, 'for now'?" Jessica asked in a dead tone.

Amy shifted uncomfortably in her seat. "Well, they won't be sure you cheated until you retake the test, right?"

"Wrong." Jessica's eyes flashed. "They can be sure now—that I'm innocent. Because I wouldn't do something as stupid as cheat on the SATs."

Pushing past Heather, she got up and went back to Ken.

"Ken, let's go to Miller's Point," Jessica said, grabbing her jacket. "Where we won't be bothered by these ignoramuses." She shot a withering glance at Heather. "Or is it ignorami?"

Chapter 9

"Liz, I really wish I could spend some time with you tonight, but with these scholarship offers coming left and right, I really need to take my studies more seriously," Todd said.

"That's exactly why I drove all the way over here," Elizabeth responded earnestly. "I need to talk to you about the SATs and college—and about our lives together."

"I'm not sure what I can do to help you, Liz," Todd said with an apologetic shrug.

"You can understand what I'm going through. Do I have to spell it out for you?" she said, her voice breaking.

Elizabeth sat down on the arm of Todd's leather chair, then took off her jacket and laid it carefully across her lap.

"I guess what you're going through is hard, Liz."

Todd distractedly opened up a book. "But I'm in the spotlight, and I've got to perform."

Elizabeth's eyes filled, and she ran her fingers through her hair. "Todd, pushing me away just isn't like you—the real you, underneath this burst into stardom."

Todd looked away from her, staring out the window of his room in the stately brick-fronted mansion. Mr. Wilkins had worked hard to earn the promotion that had made their family wealthy, and it was only natural that Todd would follow in his father's footsteps on his own path to success. He *was* a star, and he had to do whatever it took to stay on top.

He turned back to Elizabeth, watching her clasp her hands together and look questioningly at him with shiny eyes. He loved her, but what if they weren't heading in the same direction anymore?

Still, she looked so worried and confused that maybe he should give her a break. Todd was a high-level athletic scholar, but he was still the same humble and generous guy he'd always been.

"All right," he said, closing his book. "I can wait one more night before starting my new rigorous study program."

"I need your support, not your charity," Elizabeth said dryly.

"Sorry," Todd said lightly.

Elizabeth sighed. "Listen, this is serious. Some people think Jessica may have stolen my test scores," she continued, looking down at the floor. "Maybe she didn't." She looked back up again. "Then again, maybe she did."

"Well, whether she did or she didn't, the scores you received still have your name on them. They're all you've got," Todd said, checking his watch.

"Are they really all I've got? Is that all I am, a few test scores?" Her Pacific-blue eyes melted into deep, sad pools.

Memories of the many times he'd gazed into her azure eyes flashed before him. Their private walks on the beach, their candlelit dinners. He thought of times he'd waited for her at the *Oracle* office. She'd be typing furiously to finish an article, then gaze quickly up at him with joy and fire in her eyes.

"Elizabeth, you know that's not what I meant," Todd sighed. "Of course you're more than a few test scores."

Elizabeth looked unconvinced. "Well, you've got work to do. I'm sorry I've wasted your time," she said, getting up from the chair and putting on her jacket.

"Don't go yet," Todd said, running a hand through his hair. He stood up and placed his hands on her shoulders. "Let's go up to Miller's Point."

He pressed his lips softly to hers and pulled her into his arms. "See?" he said quietly. "Nothing's changed."

"I hope so," Elizabeth said, looking up at him with both love and doubt in her eyes.

。　　　。　　　。

"I'm so glad we got away from those cretins," Jessica said to Ken, cuddling close to him and feeling the cool breeze that blew into the open car window. "At least you understand me."

Ken turned the wheel of his white Toyota and pulled into Miller's Point. As he parked the car and turned off the engine, the glittering lights of Sweet Valley shone far below.

"This is definitely more like it," Ken agreed, wrapping an arm around Jessica and pulling her close to him.

He lifted her face to his, and Jessica melted into the kiss, feeling delicious heat spread through her limbs. Ken kissed her eyelids, her cheek, her throat. As she held him tightly, she opened her eyes and looked over his shoulder at the stars winking down on her, the moon shining golden and warm.

His lips found hers again, softly, then more deeply, and Jessica thought she would float into the heavens. Nothing else mattered in the whole world. Homework, parents, and people at school all faded away. Kissing Ken under a starry night was what life was all about.

After a few minutes Ken pulled away and cupped her face with his hand. "Jessica, I want to ask you something." His expression was serious.

"Anything," she whispered, gazing at his handsome face through lowered lids.

"Jess, you can tell me the truth. I promise it's just between us," he said softly.

"Truth? What truth?" Jessica asked. Her misty, love-struck eyes grew round with a vague sense of alarm.

"Did you cheat on the SATs? It's OK, honest. I mean, I can understand why you might. I just want you to tell me the truth," Ken said. She froze solid as he kissed her softly on the cheek.

"You must be joking." Jessica stared at him in shock. "Do you really think I cheated?"

"Jess, there are the school board's conclusions, and, well, everyone's been talking, and—"

"Lies," Jessica interrupted, feeling her heart squeeze painfully. "It's all gossip and lies. Haven't I said eight million times that I'm totally innocent? How can you believe all that garbage, instead of trusting my word?" Jessica leaned back against the passenger door to distance herself from Ken as much as possible.

"I didn't say I believe it. I'm just asking if . . . if any of it *might* be true," Ken said, reaching across the car for her.

She pushed him away. "You're just as bad as every-one else. You think I'm stupid just because I refuse to spend my life buried up to my ears in schoolbooks."

"I don't—"

"You don't think I could've pulled off high test scores on my own. I knew it last night, when we were at the cafe."

"Well, you even said at first that your scores weren't that great," Ken said testily. "How am I supposed to know what's true and what's not true with you?"

"I'll tell you what's true," Jessica said in a shaky

voice. "You only like me for my looks. It's never occurred to you that I have any brains."

"Jess, you're going off the deep end," Ken said with exasperation, gripping the steering wheel.

"I trusted you." Jessica shook her head with disbelief.

Jessica thought back to all the intimate conversations she'd had with Ken when she'd been going through a really bad time with Jeremy Randall. They'd even survived a nightmare camping trip in Death Valley together, when both their lives had been in serious danger. If their relationship wasn't based on mutual trust after all that, then what was the point?

She opened the car door and stepped out.

"Jessica! Get back in the car. Where are you going at this time of night?"

"I'll figure it out. I'm pretty smart," Jessica replied. "You know, I thought you were the one person who really knew me and would stand by me. I guess I was wrong."

"Please get back in the car," he pleaded.

Jessica slammed the Toyota door and leaned into the open window. "Believe what you want, Ken." She turned and walked into the blackened night.

Elizabeth parked the Jeep at Miller's Point and Todd slid near her, putting a strong arm around her shoulders. She rested her head against his chest and breathed deeply, relaxing for the first time in days. The flickering lights of Sweet Valley gave the night a magic touch.

Todd gently caressed her mouth with his finger-tips. "Your lips are so soft," he whispered as he drew her close.

He brushed Elizabeth's lips with his, and she felt the warmth of his breath as she ran her hand through his dark hair. Glancing up at the warm, glowing moonlight, she pulled back and rested quietly in his arms.

"It's so great just to be together." Elizabeth sighed with deep contentment.

"Taking a break to be with you was just what I needed, Liz," Todd said.

"It's strange how fast everything is changing," Elizabeth said, relieved at how easily she could talk to Todd again.

Todd kissed the top of her head. "That's why it's good sometimes just to sit peacefully on a dark night and watch the city lights."

Warmth and trust washed over Elizabeth, and she wondered how she could ever have thought Todd didn't care about her concerns and her future. She could tell him anything in the world—it was just a matter of finding the right time and place to talk.

"Todd, this whole situation with the SATs has been so weird," she began as she nestled closer to him.

"Oh, I know. How am I ever going to choose be-tween all the colleges that want me?" Todd responded.

Elizabeth felt her heart drop. "Todd, I need your help with this. My self-esteem has been at an all-time low. I need to feel like I still have a future."

"I'm feeling strange, too. Nervous, mostly. I mean, scouts are coming from really high-powered universities. They're all going to be focused on *me*," Todd said, pointing to his chest.

"I guess you're everyone's favorite subject these days," she said slowly.

Elizabeth sat up and moved away from him, fixing her gaze out the window. The moon was now a harsh yellow light in the sky, and she closed her eyes to shut it out. Todd barely seemed to notice that she'd unwrapped herself from his arms.

"What school should I go to, Liz? You used to know a lot about college," Todd said

You used to know a lot about college. The words felt like a bucket of cold water in her face. Todd had apparently decided that Elizabeth's future was already dead, buried, and fossilized—that is, if he was thinking about her at all.

"Don't you think I still know something about college?" she said tightly.

"The Princeton basketball coach is really great, but I've also heard good stuff about the guy at Yale," Todd went on, ignoring her question.

Elizabeth drummed her fingers on the dashboard.

"So what do you think, Liz?" Todd asked, throwing an arm around her again. "Should I go to Princeton or Yale?"

Elizabeth felt anger rising within her. She had to face the fact that Todd wasn't listening to her because he was terminally stuck on himself.

Elizabeth reached over Todd and opened the door on the passenger side.

"Get out of the car," she said.

"What?" Todd said with a blank look on his face.

"I said get out. I'm sick of your self-centered arrogance."

Todd stared at her. "Elizabeth, we're out in the middle of nowhere. I don't understand you, what did I do wrong?"

"You're totally oblivious to my feelings. So get lost," she said.

She gave him a shove with her sandals, and he tumbled out of the car, falling onto the dirt parking lot.

"Have you gone crazy?" he shouted as he stood up and brushed himself off.

"I've never been saner in my life. Have a nice walk home," Elizabeth yelled. "Or maybe one of your fancy college recruiters will pick you up."

Elizabeth pulled the door of the Jeep shut and turned the key in the ignition.

Jessica stormed across the Miller's Point parking lot, pulling her jacket shut and wondering how she was going to get home. She'd have to walk or hitchhike—but even with her normally wild lifestyle, hitchhiking was one risk she'd never take. And the last thing she planned to do was go crawling back to Ken.

A chill ran up Jessica's spine as she realized she was stranded.

She walked on in the darkness. Suddenly she

stumbled right into someone. "Who's that?" she gasped, jerking back. She squinted into the dazed face of the person she'd bumped into. "Todd? What in the world are *you* doing here?"

"I *thought* I was having a civil conversation with your sister," Todd spit out. "But she's gone completely over the edge."

"She does that sometimes. Any particular reason tonight?"

"I don't know. I was just talking about my scholarship offers, and about what school I should pick, and what a big deal this is," Todd said.

Todd blabbered on, talking about basketball coaches. Jessica rolled her eyes. He had obviously been acting like a self-centered jerk, not understanding Elizabeth's crisis any better than Ken understood Jessica's.

Jessica's heart stopped. She realized that with all the attention she'd been getting because of her high SAT scores, she hadn't even thought about how Elizabeth must feel. Her sister was such a nerdy, goody-two-shoes Girl Scout that it must have been terrible for her to have got low scores. Jessica wished she could throw her arms around Elizabeth right then.

As it is, I'll probably never even get home in one piece, she thought.

Jessica blinked at the flash of a pair of headlights. It was Elizabeth headed her way in the Jeep!

"Hey, Jess! Need a lift?" Elizabeth called out.

A tremendous wave of relief and love for her

twin swept over Jessica as she ran to the Jeep and jumped in.

Todd had found his way over to Ken, who was standing by the open door of his Toyota.

"Looks like the Wakefield girls have both gone berserk!" Ken said loudly. Todd jerked open the passenger door of the Toyota.

Jessica waved good-bye as the Jeep peeled out of Miller's Point.

"Did you see the look on Todd's face when I kicked him out of the Jeep?" Elizabeth said.

Jessica giggled. "I don't think those guys knew who they were dealing with tonight," she answered.

Elizabeth leaned back in the driver's seat, the wind caressing her face. As the Jeep sailed down the road, she watched the twinkling lights of Sweet Valley speed by. She also felt the icy tension between herself and her sister melt into the velvet night.

"I guess we're officially friends again," Jessica said with mock sulkiness.

"Until the next time I can't stand you," Elizabeth sighed, tossing Jess a quick glance.

Jessica folded her hands behind her head. "Hey, we've got the car. Let's head for the border."

"I've got a better idea. Let's head for Casey's," Elizabeth said. "Dealing with Todd's swelled ego has worn me out. I could use a root beer float."

"I'm going for a triple hot-fudge sundae," Jessica responded dreamily.

Elizabeth came to the bottom of the hill and turned right, past a row of palm trees. "Hey, Jess?" she asked.

"Yes?" Jessica answered, curling up in the passenger seat with her eyes closed.

"I'm sorry I accused you of stealing my SAT scores. I know you didn't cheat on those tests." The Jeep hummed over the road.

Jessica opened her eyes and looked at Elizabeth. "I'm sorry, too."

"For what? You didn't do anything," Elizabeth said, stopping at a red light.

"That's right. And I *should* have done something when you got your scores. I should have been there for you to talk to," Jessica said. "You obviously haven't got much support from bonehead Wilkins."

"Todd's got a lot on his mind, I guess," Elizabeth said tightly. The light turned green.

"Maybe a lot on it, but not much in it," Jessica snorted.

"Normally, I wouldn't agree. But at the moment you may have a point."

"And, by the way, Liz, I hope that dumb test didn't make you feel like you're stupid—because you're one of the smartest people at Sweet Valley High," Jessica declared.

"I'm not so sure of that anymore."

"You're *so* smart," Jessica blurted out. "You've gotten all A's in school since we could walk."

"Well, yeah, I guess I have," Elizabeth said, surprised by Jessica's outburst.

107

"I know I've never cared about school that much," Jessica continued, taking a deep breath. "But secretly I've always been jealous of you, Liz. I never thought I was as smart as you are."

Elizabeth was stunned. In ten thousand years it wouldn't have dawned on her that Jessica was jealous of her.

"Jessica, first of all you're incredibly smart. Second of all—*you're* jealous of *me*? Do you realize how jealous *I've* always been of *you*?"

"No way!" Jessica exclaimed incredulously.

"Just look at you. You breeze through life, you've got a great sense of style, you've got tons of athletic abilities, plus acting talent and real savvy about people," Elizabeth said.

"I never guessed you thought those things about me were cool," Jessica said.

"Well, guess again," Elizabeth said. "And, besides, you did incredibly well on the SATs without twisting yourself into a pretzel worrying about them. Maybe I should take a clue from that."

Jessica stared out the window. "Yeah, but look where I am now. Only you and Mom and Dad believe I got those scores honestly."

"So never mind anyone else. We'll get you through this," Elizabeth replied firmly.

"But, Elizabeth, I'm sick of everyone thinking I'm a screwup."

"I don't think you're a screwup, Jess."

"Oh, yes, you do. Everyone does—even Ken."

Jessica banged her fist down on the dashboard. "I'm going to cram for the SATs this time and get perfect scores. That'll really send everyone into shock."

Elizabeth sighed as she pulled the Jeep into a parking space in front of Casey's. Jessica sounded pretty determined about preparing for the SAT retake, but Elizabeth's whole attitude had changed. Maybe she'd get better scores and maybe she wouldn't. At this point, she really didn't care.

Chapter 10

Jessica gritted her teeth and turned the page of her math workbook. It was a Friday night, and she couldn't believe she was slaving away at her desk. But the retake of the SATs was scheduled for nine o'clock the next morning. She'd been killing herself all week studying for the test, determined to get superhigh scores and clear her name.

She stretched her arms and yawned, then pushed her bangs away from her sweaty forehead. *This must be what doing homework on a regular basis is like,* she thought. *No wonder I've never wanted any part of it.*

She got up and dug around in a mound of laundry for a sweatshirt. Elizabeth had always said Jessica's room looked like a mud-wrestling pit, but at the moment it was an even bigger mess than usual. For five days straight, Jessica had dashed home from school and done nothing but burrow into her workbooks, letting everything else fall apart.

Clothes were piled several feet high on her bed, on the rug, and on her chair. Shirts draped from her shelves and her bedside lamp. She unearthed a wrinkled football jersey and pulled it over her head, then shoved aside the dead plants and wads of crumpled-up workbook practice sheets, and plowed her way back to her desk.

"Jessica!" Mrs. Wakefield called up from the front hallway. "Winston is here."

Jessica put her pencil between her teeth and bit hard. "Send him up, Mom," she mumbled, squeezing her eyes shut.

She couldn't believe she was desperate enough to ask Winston to come over and help her study, but extreme circumstances called for extreme measures. Spending a Friday night in her room with the Sweet Valley class clown was about as extreme as it got.

"Jessica, light of my life. I thought we'd never be alone to satisfy our tormented longing for one another," Winston called as he came up the stairs. He banged on the door and burst into the room. Jessica covered her eyes with her hands so she didn't have to look at his pink Hawaiian shirt.

"Careful not to break the door down. I've grown rather fond of it," Jessica said irritably. "Besides, this is not a date, got it?" she added, waving her pencil at him. "I have to do even better on the SATs tomorrow than I did the first time. Pull up a chair and let's get to work.

"I may need some preliminary instruction on just how, exactly, to pull up a chair," Winston said, scratching his head. "It looks like a shopping mall exploded in here."

Jessica reached over and pushed an avalanche of jeans and tops off the rocking chair near her desk. "Sit."

"Your wish is my command." Winston lowered himself into the chair.

"All right, Winston, let's get down to business," Jessica said, handing him the math book. "I want to know every one of the equations in this book cold."

Winston peered at her through his glasses. "Ms. Wakefield, as your professor, I consider it my job to suggest that you take it easy."

"Take it easy? Take it easy means lying on a beach towel, slathered in coconut oil," Jessica said dryly. "This is study. In other words, torture."

"Well, it doesn't have to be," Winston said, casting her a sideways look. "Memorizing the entire book isn't necessarily the best way to prepare for the SATs."

"I see," Jessica said, tapping her pencil impatiently. "And what would you recommend?"

Winston shrugged. "You told me over the phone that you've been working pretty hard on this all week," he said. "As much as I thrill to these rare moments in your company, Jessica, I'd honestly suggest you just watch a little TV tonight and then go to bed early."

"You must think I'm an imbecile, like everyone else does," Jessica remarked sharply. "I suppose watching TV is exactly what *you* did the night before the SATs."

"Yes, that's exactly what I did," Winston replied evenly.

Jessica stared at him, confused.

"Not that studying isn't important. It can definitely help, and I did take the preparation course the week before the test," he continued. "But you don't want to overdo it. Frankly, you look like you haven't slept in a month."

"Thanks for the compliment," Jessica said testily. "By the way, that outfit is really you."

"Oh, do you like it?" he asked cheerfully, looking down at his shirt. "Anyway, you've probably memorized enough words and numbers, so why don't you chill out and relax? Want to go down and see what's on TV?" he asked hopefully.

"I plan to engage in some private chilling and relaxing after this exam is over," Jessica responded. Winston had always lusted after her, and she wasn't surprised he'd try to finagle this study session into a date. "But tonight I'm going to study my brains out. You can either help me or not," she added tightly.

"Suit yourself," Winston said, shaking his head. He glanced at his watch. "I can hang out and drill you for about an hour. I'm kind of thirsty, though. Is it OK if I get a soda or something first?"

"Yeah," Jessica said with a sigh. "Go down and help yourself."

Winston got up and waded through the swamp of

clothes. He stopped in the doorway and turned around. "Oh, by the way, Jessica," he said in a chirpy voice, snapping his fingers as if he'd just remembered something.

"What now?" Jessica said dully.

"I don't think you're an imbecile," he said quietly. Then he disappeared down the stairs.

She turned her head abruptly toward the empty doorway, then stared back at her workbook. Her reputation was at stake, and she needed to prove herself to people who mattered a lot more than Winston Egbert.

Jessica decided she wasn't going to sleep at all. She was determined to study furiously all night long, right until it was time to take the test.

"Where's your new silk shirt? I want to borrow it," Elizabeth asked as she breezed into Jessica's room.

The test was early the next morning, and Elizabeth felt great. She'd spent the afternoon lounging on the couch, eating oranges and frozen yogurt and reading a mystery novel. Now she was getting ready to go out to a film festival.

"If you can find it, it's yours," Jessica grumbled into her workbook. "But if you spill anything on it, I'll kill you."

Elizabeth sailed over to the closet, threw open the doors, and pawed through everything until she found the shirt.

"Mom always says I look good in this bright-coral

color," Elizabeth said, holding the top to her chest and admiring herself in Jessica's full-length mirror. "By the way, I like your room like this. It's so . . . so creative."

"Did somebody steal my sister and leave you here as an impostor?" Jessica asked. She arched an eyebrow.

"Nope, same old sister. I've just had the best week of my life. I hung out on the beach yesterday afternoon and finally read *The Color Purple,* which I've been meaning to do for ages."

"Did you at least spend last night studying for the SATs?" Jessica asked with alarm.

"Last night Enid and I went to Bobo's Burger Barn. It's the most fun place. You can draw on the tablecloths, and they give you a balloon when you leave." She pulled one of Jessica's slinky satin dresses out of the closet.

"Sounds cool," Jessica said with a puzzled expression. "Where'd you get those Italian sandals? I don't think I've seen them before."

"Oh, these. Well, I spent Wednesday afternoon shopping at the Valley Mall. I just couldn't resist them," Elizabeth bubbled.

"Shopping? Sunbathing? Bobo's?" Jessica said incredulously. "Earth to Elizabeth. We are taking the SATs tomorrow morning. Aren't you a little concerned about that?"

Elizabeth had located Jessica's hats and was trying them all on. "Why should I be concerned? I'm not wasting any energy worrying about that," she said. "Have you ever noticed what an interesting place the mall is? So many different people and sounds and colors and—"

"I prefer to focus on the clothes," Jessica interrupted impatiently. "Look, if you're not going to study, would you mind taking the fashion show elsewhere, so I can?"

"Jess, I mean it. There's so much to learn from just settling back and watching people." Elizabeth sat down in the rocking chair by Jessica's desk. It was the only place in the room that didn't have clothes all over it. "It's just as much a part of our education as facts and tests."

"This is fascinating. Now, would you get lost so I can study?" Jessica said with annoyance. "You may have given up on the SATs, but I'm still determined to make a spectacular showing."

Elizabeth shrugged. Maybe she'd suggest to Mr. Collins that she write her special essay about an ordinary afternoon at the Valley Mall. She'd talk to him about the idea next week and then get right to work on it.

"See you later," Elizabeth said. She leaped over a pile of jeans to get out the door, sat down by the hall phone, and dialed Enid's number.

"Hello?"

"Hi, Enid, it's me, Liz. There's a short animation film playing downtown that I really want to see. Let's go."

"What's got into you in the last few days, Liz?" Enid asked, with concern in her voice. "Aren't you worried about the SATs? You've done nothing all week but shop, lie on the beach, and read."

"And wait until I tell you about the book I started today," Elizabeth said, twirling a strand of hair around her finger. "It's about this woman who grew up on a sheep farm in the Australian outback and eventually went to Harvard. By the way, whose turn is it to buy popcorn?"

Saturday afternoon, Jessica was lying comatose on the couch underneath a patchwork quilt, listlessly watching an afternoon B movie. She was too burned out even to eat the sandwich lying on the plate next to her.

"What's the matter, don't you like the gourmet cuisine I made for you? It's my pastrami special," Elizabeth said, walking energetically into the living room. "I'd think you'd be famished after finishing the SATs."

"It looks great," Jessica said unenthusiastically. "I'm just too tired to eat."

Elizabeth placed a hand on Jessica's forehead. "Too tired to eat? Is this the same Jessica Wakefield who can fly into the Dairi Burger after a rigorous cheerleading practice and chomp down a double cheeseburger, fries, and a vanilla shake?"

"When have I ever had that much energy? I don't remember," Jessica said lethargically.

"I'm not surprised that you're this exhausted," Elizabeth said. "Listen, I know a great way to revive you."

"Liz, just let me die right here," Jessica said, staring at the TV with glazed eyes.

Elizabeth knelt down by the couch and blocked Jessica's view of the television.

"How about driving down with me to the Sweet Valley Marina? Nicholas Morrow has his boat moored down there, and he wants to take us sailing." Elizabeth's eyes were glistening.

Jessica turned over on her stomach and groaned. Then she propped herself on her elbow and tried to see the TV commercial over Elizabeth's head.

"Liz, how can you be so disgustingly cheerful? Aren't you even concerned about the test?" Jessica asked.

Elizabeth shrugged. "I just want to put the SATs behind us, so we can get on with our lives. Besides, I'm sure you did fine."

"I don't want to see anyone. I just want to spend the weekend catching up on sleep," Jessica said, covering her face with her hands.

Elizabeth shoved Jessica's legs over on the couch and sat down.

"Now it's *my* sister who's been stolen, with an impostor left in her place." Elizabeth peeled Jessica's fingers away from her face and peered down at her. "When have you ever turned down an opportunity to spend an afternoon anywhere near the beach?"

Jessica pulled the quilt up over her head.

"We'll go to the Beach Disco tonight and dance," Elizabeth added enticingly. "Come on, what's with you? This isn't the first time you've stayed up all night."

Jessica always waited until the last minute to start her homework, so she'd often stayed up until all hours to finish school projects. Still, it was rare for her not to have energy to burn on the dance floor the next night.

She knew she wasn't just tired; she felt pinned to the couch with lead weights because she was depressed. If she didn't score high again, she wouldn't graduate with everyone else, which would be the humiliation of the century.

"I just want to be left alone," Jessica finally said.

Elizabeth nodded and pushed herself up from the couch. "Well, I'll give you a call after we come in from the boat to see if you've changed your mind about dancing."

Jessica watched Elizabeth grab her windbreaker and check herself in the mirror. She took the barrettes out of her hair, shook loose the waves of blond silk, and flew out the door.

Jessica sank back into the pillows. *I've never seen Elizabeth relax and enjoy life so much*, she thought morosely. She flipped through the channels, then turned the TV off and stared at the ceiling, her chest aching. She'd rather hide in a cave for the rest of her life than show up at the Beach Disco that night.

I can't face anyone until I get my new test scores and I'm thoroughly vindicated. I've got to prove that everyone was wrong about me. Jessica turned over and buried her face in the couch.

Chapter 11

Weeks later . . .

"Turn to page fifteen in your textbooks," Ms. Rice said to the first-period health class on Friday morning. "Today we're going to discuss the importance of diet, exercise, and rest. We'll begin with the four basic food groups."

The last thing I feel like doing is listening to a lecture on good health, Jessica thought. She'd barely eaten or slept in the weeks since she'd retaken the SATs. She knew she'd get the results any day, and she was starting to get jumpy.

"I'd say you've come to the right place," Lila whispered from the desk behind Jessica. "You look like you could use an infusion of health."

"I'm so nervous, I can hardly sit still," Jessica whispered back. She was tapping her foot on the floor and her pen on the desk.

Ms. Rice stopped listing grain and dairy products on the board and spun quickly around. "Who is creating so much disturbance?" She rested her gaze on Jessica, who had frozen into a statue. "There will be a quiz on this material on Monday," she said, arching an eyebrow. "Which should be of importance to *most* of you." Ms. Rice turned around again and faced the blackboard.

"Don't worry about Rice. She's just got a hawk eye for anyone who's not in peak condition," Lila whispered. "By the way, the dark circles under your eyes are very chic. They give you that dangerous, hungry look."

"Thanks a lot, I've been working on an image makeover," Jessica whispered back.

Jessica brushed her fingers through her limp hair and across her pale skin. *I can't take the stress of waiting much longer,* she thought.

Ms. Rice was looking at the board, pointing to words with a piece of white chalk. "Every day it's important to eat four servings of grains and pasta, and two servings of cooked green vegetables."

"That's what I probably look like right now," Jessica whispered to Lila. "Cooked green vegetables."

"I have the only antidote known to humankind."

Jessica heard her friend scribbling on paper behind her; then Lila handed her a note. Jessica unfolded the torn piece of notebook paper and saw the word "shopping" scrawled in huge letters across the middle of the page.

Normally, that word would have sent spasms of electric excitement through Jessica's body, but today she was too worried about her scores to enjoy thinking about clothes.

Jessica twisted around and handed the paper back to Lila. When she turned again to face the front of the classroom, Ms. Rice was standing in front of Jessica's desk, her arms folded across her chest.

"I'd like to see a little more attention paid to the lesson and a little less to socializing," Ms. Rice said. "Especially you, Jessica. You're apparently walking on thin ice, as it is."

Jessica felt the heat rise in her face as the entire class turned to stare at her.

I won't be on thin ice much longer, you bag of root vegetables. The truth will set me free, Jessica wanted to say. But the words caught in her throat.

There was a light knock at the classroom door, and Ms. Rice walked over to answer it. She spoke in low tones to a student who Jessica knew worked in the principal's office, then turned around to face the class.

"Everyone start reading the study questions for the next chapter, and we'll talk about them in a few minutes," she instructed.

As people opened their books and shuffled through the pages, Ms. Rice walked to the back of the room and leaned quietly over Jessica's shoulder.

"Jessica, please go straight to Mr. Cooper's office. Your SAT scores are in."

◦　　◦　　◦

"Hi, Rosemary," Jessica said confidently to Chrome Dome's secretary.

"Hello, Jessica," Rosemary said. She rolled a fresh sheet of paper into her typewriter. "You can go on in. You look a little tired, dear."

"I'm fine," Jessica said. She opened Mr. Cooper's office door and marched in. She smiled at Elizabeth, who was already seated.

Jessica froze in her tracks when she saw her parents sitting in chairs next to the large desk. Her stomach leaped into her throat at the sight of their questioning expressions. *Well, they're probably just as anxious as I am to find out what the new scores are,* she told herself.

"Mom, Dad, what a surprise to see you here," Jessica said with an effort at cheerfulness. She shot a glance at Elizabeth, who looked just as surprised.

"Won't you join us, Jessica? We'll make this gathering as brief as possible," Mr. Cooper said, gesturing toward a chair next to Elizabeth.

Jessica sat down and started chewing her thumbnail.

"Well, I think we can get straight down to business," Chrome Dome said, leaning forward across his desk. "Your parents have already been informed of your test results."

Jessica looked quickly at her parents and tried desperately to read their expressions. They didn't look angry, which was a good sign, but they weren't exactly turning cartwheels.

123

"How did I do?" Jessica asked them. Her father looked at Mr. Cooper, raising both eyebrows. She felt a sense of doom start to rise in the pit of her stomach.

"Not very well, I'm afraid," Chrome Dome said in a tired voice. He picked up a piece of paper from his desktop and adjusted his glasses.

Jessica's heart was pounding in her ears.

Chrome Dome cleared his throat and looked meaningfully at each member of the Wakefield family.

Spare the dramatics and just read the scores, Jessica thought, groaning inwardly.

"Jessica, you've scored four-forty in math, and four-seventy in the verbal section." He turned to Elizabeth. "Liz, you've achieved impressive scores of seven-fifty verbal and seven-twenty math."

"What?" Jessica said, feeling the room swirl. "How . . . ? But . . ."

Elizabeth gasped and stared incredulously at Jessica. *This can't be happening,* Jessica thought as she felt the color drain from every inch of her body.

She shook her head in disbelief and turned to her parents. "Mom, I don't understand," Jessica stammered. Mrs. Wakefield nodded, and her eyes filled with sympathy.

"I'm not surprised Liz aced the tests the second time, Mr. Cooper. But there must be some mistake with my scores," Jessica declared.

"I don't think that's likely, Jessica. In fact, this is really all the proof the school board needs."

"All the proof they need for what?" Jessica asked,

trying to keep her voice from trembling as the sensation of doom now wrapped itself around her body like a snake.

"That you cheated on the first set of SATs," Chrome Dome answered. "Frankly, I'm quite disappointed. Despite your lack of academic enthusiasm, I've always had the highest regard for your school spirit."

"Mr. Cooper," Mr. Wakefield interrupted in a quiet but firm voice. "I think Jessica is feeling some shock over this. Please just tell us what happens next."

"As you wish," Mr. Cooper said, nodding his head. "Jessica is temporarily suspended, pending a meeting with the school board. She may face permanent expulsion."

Jessica closed her eyes, wishing she could open them and be a million miles away. She'd wanted so many times to blow off school for good, but now the thought of being kicked out of all her classes filled her with dread. *I'll be a social outcast,* she thought, gripping the arms of her chair.

"And it goes without saying that you are also suspended from the cheerleading squad until further notice," Mr. Cooper continued.

Jessica felt as if she'd been hit in the solar plexus. She could hardly breathe. She'd bullied Heather into letting her cheer during the last few weeks, but now she didn't have a prayer.

"Now, just a minute. These penalties are harsh and shortsighted," Mrs. Wakefield said.

"I agree," Mr. Wakefield added. "Besides, the

reversal on these tests doesn't necessarily prove that Jessica cheated on the first set."

Chrome Dome folded his hands on the desk. "Mr. and Mrs. Wakefield, I appreciate your concern. But the school board has made its position clear. There's really nothing I can do."

Jessica closed her eyes again, wishing her parents wouldn't argue with Mr. Cooper. She wanted to go home and lock herself in her room.

"No, I think there may be a great deal we can all do," Mr. Wakefield countered. "If the school board is willing to seek a creative solution to this problem."

"With all due respect to your highly regarded place in our community, Mr. Wakefield, your daughter has cheated on a national exam of critical importance," Mr. Cooper responded.

"How do you really know?" Elizabeth suddenly blurted out. Jessica stared at her with red-rimmed eyes. "Don't you think you should be able to prove this beyond a shadow of a doubt before you ruin my sister's life?"

"Elizabeth," Mrs. Wakefield said gently, placing a hand on her daughter's arm.

"No, Mom, it's not fair," Elizabeth insisted. "None of this is fair."

Jessica couldn't stand to sit there and listen to this pointless bickering any longer. The room suddenly felt so stifling, she thought she might faint. She pushed back her chair with a loud scrape and stood up.

"I guess there's nothing more to discuss," Jessica

said with great dignity. She turned to her family. "Mom, Dad, Liz—I'll see you at home."

Jessica strode across the office as Chrome Dome gaped at her.

"Young lady, I don't think we've formally concluded this meeting," he said, flustered.

Jessica stopped at the doorway, nodded graciously to him, and stepped outside the office. She quietly shut the door behind her.

" 'Bye, Rosemary," Jessica said pleasantly as she headed out of the main office.

"Good-bye, dear."

Out in the hallway, Jessica braced herself against the wall. She was breathing hard, fighting back nausea.

I'm going to spend the rest of my life as a high-school dropout, she thought miserably. *My sixteen years on the planet have come to nothing.*

Chapter 12

"Meeting the Friday-morning deadline—that's what I like to see," Mr. Collins said, leaning over Elizabeth's shoulder.

Elizabeth squinted at her computer screen. "I'll print this out for you in just a second, Mr. Collins."

She typed in the last sentence of her "Personal Profiles" column, nodded with satisfaction, and pressed the print command.

"It's good to see you back up to speed, Elizabeth."

"I'm feeling a little better. Thanks for all your help," she responded, smiling at her favorite teacher.

"I'd think you'd be feeling *a lot* better, with such a strong showing on your second SATs," he said with a grin.

"Well, it's certainly a relief," she replied. *It would be even more of a relief if my sister weren't hanging out on a street corner right now,* she added silently.

Elizabeth stood up and walked to the laser printer to get her finished "Profiles" piece. She picked it up, scanned quickly down the page, and handed the paper to Mr. Collins.

He sat down on the edge of her desk, scrutinizing the writing. "Nice job, Liz. Now, what subject have you chosen for your special editorial assignment?"

"What if I wrote about a typical afternoon in the Valley Mall?" Elizabeth asked as she took her seat again. "I could interview random store owners and shoppers about their day."

"Sounds interesting," Mr. Collins commented. "Do you have a unifying theme to pull it all together?"

Elizabeth leaned her chin in her palm and thought for a second. "The idea would be that people may seem a certain way on the surface, but once you get to know them a little, they might have many sides to them."

Mr. Collins nodded. "Sounds good. It'll sharpen your interviewing skills and give you a chance to explore an important idea."

"Great," Elizabeth said. She smiled broadly as she watched Mr. Collins walk to the other side of the room.

"Hey, Liz, let's talk about layout for that editorial you're working on," Olivia Davidson called, walking up to Elizabeth's workstation. "Penny told me about your new story idea—it's really creative. I want to try something new in the design." She pulled up a chair next to Elizabeth. "Is it OK if Allen Walters goes with you to the mall and takes some photographs?"

"Sure, that would be fun," Elizabeth said.

"By the way, you must be happy that your SATs are up," Olivia said. "You never said exactly what you got the first time, but I knew you were feeling pretty down about them." Olivia made a line count on the terminal next to Elizabeth's and jotted some numbers down on a piece of paper. "I'm not surprised your scores improved."

"You're not?" Elizabeth asked.

"Of course I'm not." Olivia looked up at Elizabeth. "Is that such a shock?"

Elizabeth looked down at her hands. "I don't know, Olivia. I guess I was starting to wonder if I was really smart or not."

"Are you kidding? Liz, everyone who crosses your path knows how smart you are. That first test was obviously a fluke. You were having a bad day. So what?" Olivia said, putting the paper in a folder and heading back to her design table.

Elizabeth stared at her computer monitor. Olivia didn't bat an eyelash at the fluctuations of Elizabeth's SATs. But people questioned Jessica's high scores because they didn't expect her to do very well on a test.

If my scores could vary so dramatically, why couldn't Jessica's? Elizabeth glanced at the clock. It was almost noon. Normally, Jessica would be heading out onto the athletic field for an hour of cheerleading practice. Where was she instead? Wandering aimlessly through the mall? Melting her brain in front of a soap opera? Crying alone on a park bench? She deserved to be in school with her friends.

Anger began to stir in Elizabeth as she thought about how unfair it was that Jessica's best scores had been taken away from her. She had to prove her twin's innocence.

If only Elizabeth could talk about this problem with Todd. She used to love it when they put their heads together to solve tough problems. But just the thought of Todd sent a terrible wave of loneliness through her chest.

Ever since that night at Miller's Point when she'd kicked him out of the Jeep, Elizabeth and Todd had been stiff and awkward with each other. They hadn't officially broken up, but it was only a matter of time—unless she apologized and really talked to him about why she'd been so upset.

And she wanted desperately to feel Todd wrapping his arms around her proudly when she told him her new SAT scores.

"Let's work on the double-line formation cheer," Heather Mallone called out.

Jessica was standing thirty yards away, at the edge of the athletic field. Heather was certainly wasting no time in filling the gap left by Jessica's absence.

The squad lined up in two rows led by Jeanie West and Sandy Bacon.

"All right, one . . . two . . . three!" Heather yelled.

Jeanie and Sandy kicked up their right legs and

then leaned into their hips in a funky jazz step. Jessica remembered when she'd made up that cheer for the Big Mesa game, before Heather had even come to Sweet Valley and muscled her way onto the squad. Watching Heather, Jessica clenched her fists so tightly, she felt the circulation cut off.

Jessica squinted up into the sun. The warm crystal-blue sky and singing birds only heightened the chill of isolation she felt in her heart. It seemed as if every creature in the world belonged somewhere, except for her. It was so unfair.

She wasn't even supposed to be on the school grounds. But she had nowhere else to go. Besides, most of her friends were on the cheering squad, and she desperately needed to talk to Amy and Maria.

Maybe she'd ask the two of them to come to a slumber party at her house. They could make lemonade and nachos and go sit out by the pool at midnight. Then Jessica could tell them her side of the whole story, and they'd reassure her that she was still on the squad in spirit and still their good friend, no matter what.

"Take five minutes!" Heather called. The grating sound of her voice made Jessica flinch.

Jessica saw Amy catch sight of her, say something to Maria, and then jog over to the edge of the field.

"So what are your new SAT scores?" Amy asked, panting. She wiped her sweaty hair from her forehead and rested her hand on her knees.

"They're not that good. In fact, they're pretty low," Jessica said.

Amy leaned over and stretched her left hamstring. "What do you think happened? You studied like a maniac all week."

"I don't know. Maybe my first scores were just a fluke," Jessica said. She kicked the ground. "Or maybe I unconsciously used my psychic twin power to sap Elizabeth's brain cells during the first SATs."

"Jess, fess up. Did you actually cheat? Did you steal Elizabeth's test?" Amy asked, stretching her arms over her head.

Jessica stared at Amy. She felt hollow inside.

"No, I didn't," Jessica said in an offended tone.

"Amy, let's go, we've got a lot of work to do!" Heather called impatiently.

"Amy, please, I'm innocent. You've got to stick by me. My friends are all I've got left," Jessica pleaded. "The school board won't let me cheer. They won't even let me come to school right now." Her eyes filled with tears.

"Jess, I have to go," Amy said evenly. "Look, I'm really sorry about how all of this has turned out." Amy turned to jog back to the field.

"Amy, wait!" Jessica said. "I'll call you, OK? Maybe we can go out and do something. If you knew the whole story, it would make sense."

Amy put her hands on her hips and looked out into the field. Heather was vigorously waving for her to hurry up.

"I don't think you should call me, Jessica. It's probably not a good idea. I'm sorry," Amy said. "Take care of yourself, OK?" She headed back to the squad.

"Amy! Wait!" Jessica called, but Amy kept going. Slowly, Jessica sank to her knees in the grassy field. As the squad began practicing splits and cartwheels, she quickly brushed a single tear from her cheek.

She looked toward the other end of the playing field and saw Ken jogging in his gold gym shorts with his shirt off. Jessica hadn't spoken to him since that awful night at Miller's Point, when she'd walked out on him. But she needed more than anything for him to hold her right now.

Suddenly Jessica couldn't stop the flood of hot tears that slid down her face.

Elizabeth waited by the gym doorway, underneath a big banner advertising the game that night. She was watching Todd shoot layups. It was lunchtime on Friday, and this was the only chance she'd have all day to talk to him.

She watched him speed down the court, his long, muscular legs taking quick, deft strides. He flew up under the basket and sank the ball into the hoop.

"Look at Wilkins do his magic out there," Elizabeth heard Aaron say in the hall behind her.

"He's incredible. Aren't a lot of recruiters coming to see him tonight?" Barry asked.

"Yeah," Aaron said. "He'll have them all eating out of his hand."

Elizabeth felt a sting of irritation at the mention of the recruiters. She'd definitely heard enough about how every basketball coach in the country was begging Todd to come to his school.

Coach Tilman was pacing up and down the court. "Todd, let me see that jump shot again. Come on, do it right. You've got a lot riding on tonight's game," he yelled.

Todd was bent over, breathing hard and resting one hand on his knee. He stood up, sweat streaming from his face.

"Let's go, star," Coach Tilman called out. "Don't get tired on me now."

Todd dribbled over to the foul line, set his feet in position, and took his shot. He gracefully flicked his wrists, and the ball sank neatly into the basket.

Elizabeth watched his artful movements, feeling a jolt of pride in spite of herself. She knew that Todd was the best player in their high-school league.

She caught his eye and waved, giving him a big smile. But he just threw her an exasperated look. Tears welled up in Elizabeth's eyes and she bit her lip. She and Todd might not have been getting along well recently, but that was no excuse for him to treat her as if she were a stranger.

Todd said something to Coach Tilman and dribbled the ball over to Elizabeth.

"Hi, you look great out there," Elizabeth said.

"Hi," he said. "What's up? I don't have a lot of time."

"Uhm, I know," Elizabeth said. "Look, I'm sorry

about Miller's Point. I was upset," she began.

"Forget it, it's OK," he said brusquely. "Is that all? Because I have to go practice my free throw."

Elizabeth felt a stab of pain at his abruptness. "You've practiced hard for weeks. Can't you take just a short break?" she asked, trying to keep her voice steady. "I mean, so you won't be too tired for the game." She wished she could take him aside for just ten minutes and talk more privately.

Todd wiped the sweat from his brow. "The college talent scouts will be there. What I do on the court tonight has got to impress them."

"Todd, something terrible has happened, and I need your help," Elizabeth said firmly.

"Sorry, Liz, I just don't have time right now. Tonight could really take me somewhere," Todd replied.

Her heart contracted. Apparently, he didn't care that her only sister was about to be expelled. But he could at least take the time to hear about her own news.

"Todd, our test results came back today," she said, taking a deep breath. "I got a seven-fifty verbal and almost as high in math."

"That's great," he said, clapping her on the shoulder. "I have to go. Take it easy, OK?" He dribbled the ball back out to the court.

Elizabeth stood in the doorway and blinked. *Take it easy?* Was she supposed to be merely one of his fans? Who did he think he was?

"Todd Wilkins is such an awesome basketball player," a freshman girl said dreamily.

"I know, and he's so *cute*," added a sophomore girl.

Elizabeth was usually happy to hear people she didn't know praise Todd's basketball talent—even when it came to the younger girls, who all had huge crushes on him. But now she just felt alone and apart from the frenzy of basketball conversations she heard echoing through the halls.

But my problems are pretty tame compared to Jessica's, she thought. Todd was obviously not going to be much help in figuring out a plan to prove her innocence, so Elizabeth would have to come up with something on her own.

But what?

Chapter 13

"Don't you love listening to Mr. Collins do a dramatic reading?" Enid whispered. She leaned her chin in her hands. "There's nothing else I'd rather do on a Friday afternoon."

"Uh-huh," Elizabeth said, bringing her attention back to the classroom. She loved their English class, too, but she was having a hard time focusing on the play they were discussing. Her thoughts kept drifting to Jessica.

Mr. Collins was reading aloud from sections of *Inherit the Wind*, a play based on the true story of the trial of a schoolteacher, named Scopes, who wanted to teach his students in creative and unconventional ways.

Mr. Collins paced the aisles of the classroom with excitement. "So the lawyer in this play, Clarence Darrow, is saying that bad laws are like diseases. They destroy everything they touch."

"But they're laws. Don't you have to do what they say, no matter what?" asked Michael Schmidt.

"An excellent question," Mr. Collins said. He stopped pacing and propped a foot on an empty chair. "It's because of that very question that many people believe this is one of the most important plays written in the twentieth century."

Elizabeth had been absently drawing pictures in her notebook, wondering what Jessica was doing. But now she looked up.

"All right, you've all read the play as homework. Let's open up discussion," Mr. Collins said, walking back to the front of the room and sitting on top of his desk. "Who can tell me what Darrow says is really on trial? Barry?"

Barry took a deep breath and leaned back in his chair. "The law itself? The rules?" he guessed.

"OK, the authority that made the rules and cast the charges against Scopes is being questioned," Mr. Collins said, his eyes lighting up. He loosened his tie. "Good, Barry. But what does Darrow actually say is *on trial*?"

"The right to think," Winston called out.

"The right to think!" Mr. Collins repeated, bringing his hand down on the desk with a bang.

Elizabeth's attention was riveted. Looking down, she noticed her play was still closed in front of her. She opened it and turned to the page where the trial began.

"And what does Mr. Darrow say he actually intends

to *defend* in this trial? Enid, let's hear from you."

"This is my favorite part. It's right here," she said, pointing to the page. "He says he's defending Scopes's right to be different."

Mr. Collins leaped off the desk. "The right to be different! Isn't that what our country is based on?" He walked between the rows of chairs, peering directly at each student. "And Clarence Darrow isn't interested in arbitrary rules. What is he really interested in, Jade?"

"He's interested in truth," Jade Wu said.

"Truth," Mr. Collins said in a whisper. He stopped walking and looked slowly around the room, nodding his head.

His gaze rested on Elizabeth. She was mesmerized by the magic of the classroom discussion. This play had so much power to wake people up, how could she ever have doubted that she wanted to be a writer?

Elizabeth also realized that a good lawyer has her own kind of power. And Scopes's own testimony was so moving, there was no way the jury wouldn't have been swayed.

"When Scopes gets up to give his testimony, he apologizes that he's not a public speaker, only a schoolteacher—" Mr. Collins began.

"And everyone knows that no schoolteacher can string a coherent sentence together," Winston interrupted. The whole class, including Mr. Collins, laughed.

"Right," Mr. Collins said with a grin, the corners of his eyes crinkling. "Well, there's an exception to every rule, and Scopes was it. He strung many elegant sentences together." Mr. Collins grew serious again. "Scopes was up against a powerful opposition. But he stood his ground against what he believed was an unjust law, and he won."

He turned his back on the class and wrote the word "truth" on the blackboard in big letters. Facing the class again, he pointed to the word.

"Remember that things—and people—are usually more complicated than they seem," Mr. Collins said. "You live in a society in which you always have the right to question circumstances where the truth has been twisted or suppressed. You can do this no matter how strong the forces that oppose you might be. All it takes is commitment, and courage."

People were stirring restlessly in their seats, and the entire room felt charged with energy. Every fiber in Elizabeth's body was alive.

Question circumstances where the truth has been twisted . . . commitment and courage.

Suddenly Elizabeth had an idea.

"That's why my wash is brighter!" a toothy actress said. Jessica kept flipping the channels past commercials for dog food and laundry detergent. She found a few soap operas, a talk show. It was Friday-afternoon dullsville.

Jessica didn't have the energy to get off the couch

and find something else to do. Every ounce of her body felt dead. All she could manage was to mope around the house, watching TV and eating ice cream. She didn't even feel like shopping, since she never wanted to show her face in public again.

She was polishing off her third bowl of Rocky Road when the doorbell rang. Setting the bowl down on the coffee table and wrapping the quilt around her, Jessica dragged herself into the front hall.

She pulled open the door and dropped her jaw when she saw Ken smiling shyly at her.

"Ken!" Jessica exclaimed. She'd never been so glad to see anyone in her life.

Then she blushed, realizing that she was standing there in a quilt, with her hair all over the place. "I must look terrible," she said.

"You're beautiful." He brought his arm out from behind his back and handed her a gorgeous bouquet of flowers.

Jessica gasped. "That's so sweet! I can't believe you did this!" She threw her arms around him. "Roses, my favorite. Come in and have some ice cream."

They walked into the living room and sat down on the couch.

"Specialty of the house," she said, offering him her carton of ice cream and a spoon.

Ken put a big bite of it in his mouth. "Mmmm, this is great."

"Rocky Road," she explained cheerfully. For a few moments she watched him as he ate in silence.

"Ken, I was so awful to you at Miller's Point," Jessica finally said.

"No, it was my fault," Ken responded quickly, staring into the ice-cream carton. "I'm really sorry I doubted you. I just want you to know that I'm on your side. I know you didn't cheat on the SATs."

"You do?" Jessica said, catching her breath.

He set the carton and the spoon down on the coffee table. "In the back of my mind, I always knew you got those scores on your own. I guess I had a hard time dealing with it."

"Why, because I'm not supposed to be smart?" Jessica asked sulkily. She leaned back against the couch with a deep sigh. Then she picked up the remote control and turned the TV back on.

Ken grabbed the remote and turned the TV off again. "No," he said firmly, taking her by the shoulders and looking directly into her eyes. "Because you *are* smart." He gently rubbed her shoulders and dropped his gaze. "Smarter than *I* am."

"What?" Jessica asked, dazed.

"I always thought deep down that you were smarter than me, even though you constantly blew off school," Ken said quietly. "Maybe I was even a little jealous. It's hard to have a girlfriend who's so intelligent."

Jessica caressed Ken's cheek and pulled his face to hers in a kiss. "Of course I'm smart. I fell in love with you, didn't I?" she cooed.

"Then you forgive me for letting my ego get the best of me?" he asked hopefully.

"I'd already forgiven you. But I'm glad you came over to talk to me. I needed someone else to help me with this quart of Rocky Road."

Ken laughed softly. "Jess, no matter what Chrome Dome or anyone else says, I believe in your innocence."

Jessica wrapped her arms around Ken and held him tightly. Then she pulled back and brought her lips to his in a deep kiss that sent electric shivers through her arms and into her fingertips.

"So can I take you to the big game tonight?" Ken asked.

"Oh, the game," Jessica groaned, burying her head in his shoulder. Jessica wasn't crazy about watching Heather lead the cheerleaders solo.

"People at school would be glad to see you," Ken said.

"I'm not so sure of that." Jessica stared off into the distance, remembering how Amy had shut her out earlier that day.

"I'd love to go to the game with you tonight. But I'll have to let you know later," Jessica said.

"Why can't you let me know now?" Ken asked urgently. "I want to be with you tonight."

"I want to be with you, too," she said, touching his face with her fingertips. "But I've been kicked out of school. It might be stupid, but it's a fact." Jessica sighed. "There's the minor matter of my parents, and the major possibility that I'm grounded forever."

∘　　∘　　∘

"Someone pass me that delicious-looking lasagna," Mr. Wakefield said. "I don't like calling meetings on an empty stomach."

Jessica passed her father the glass casserole. Her hands were shaking so much, she was afraid she might drop the whole dish in his lap. The irresistible aroma of Parmesan cheese, oregano, and sauce swirled around the table, but Jessica's stomach was too tied up in knots to eat.

Mr. and Mrs. Wakefield had said that both Elizabeth and Jessica had to be at the dinner table promptly at six o'clock for a family conference.

"Jess, your mother and I have talked over your situation," Mr. Wakefield began. He broke open a roll and sliced a pat of butter with his knife.

"And?" Jessica asked calmly, twisting her napkin in her lap.

"We've decided we want you to know one thing," Mrs. Wakefield said, putting salad on her plate, then passing the bowl to Elizabeth.

Jessica shut her eyes. *They think I'm a worthless juvenile delinquent. They'll confine me to my room for a hundred years and then banish me from the family.*

"We've never doubted your integrity about your SAT tests, Jessica," Mrs. Wakefield continued.

"And we promise that somehow the family will help you through this," her father added.

Jessica's eyes snapped open.

"In the meantime, Liz will bring home your

assignments. And for once you'll have *plenty* of time to do them," Mrs. Wakefield said.

Elizabeth reached over and squeezed Jessica's arm. Mr. and Mrs. Wakefield rose from their seats and came around to Jessica's side of the table.

"We're behind you all the way," Mrs. Wakefield said, giving Jessica a big hug and then sitting back down again.

"A hundred percent," Mr. Wakefield added. He embraced Jessica tightly.

"Hey, doesn't the homework-delivery person get a hug, too?" Elizabeth objected.

"Absolutely," Mr. and Mrs. Wakefield said at the same time. They both jumped up from the table and took turns putting their arms around Elizabeth.

Jessica felt tremendous love flowing through her, the way she always did at family celebrations.

Mr. and Mrs. Wakefield sat down again and resumed eating. Jessica felt her stomach unwind. She served herself a healthy portion of lasagna, salad, and bread.

"Taking a break from your diet of Rocky Road?" Elizabeth inquired innocently.

"It's only a break, mind you," Jessica answered with her mouth full.

"Just checking."

"Mom, Dad, does this mean I can go to the basketball game with Ken tonight?" Jessica asked meekly.

Mr. and Mrs. Wakefield exchanged glances. "No

reason why not," Jessica's mother said. "As long as you spend some time this weekend on homework."

Jessica took another helping of salad. "Thanks, Mom. I'll call Ken as soon as we're done with dinner."

"Well, since we're all in such a good mood, I've got some news," Elizabeth announced.

"I'm always up for news." Mr. Wakefield looked at Elizabeth expectantly.

"I have a plan to clear Jessica's name."

"This *is* news," Mrs. Wakefield said. Jessica stared at her sister.

"I want to ask Mr. Cooper for a mock trial, in which Jessica's guilt or innocence will be decided," Elizabeth explained.

"And who's going to be the lawyer?" Jessica asked.

Elizabeth pointed to her chest. "I will. And we'll get six students and six faculty who don't know you to be the jury."

"You'd make a decent lawyer, Liz," Jessica conceded, arching an eyebrow. "At least you can't make things any worse for me at school than they are now."

"Thanks for your faith in me," Elizabeth said. "But I'm serious. I think it's the best way to see that you get fair treatment, Jess."

Elizabeth looked back at her parents. "The terms will be that if we lose, Jessica has to face the school board. But if we win, then Mr. Cooper has to back Jessica and tell the school board she's innocent."

Jessica's eyes lit up. "It sounds like a great idea. I'll be back on the cheerleading squad in no time."

"And you'd also get to go back to school, keep your original SAT scores, and graduate with the rest of the class," Elizabeth pointed out.

"We'll make a great team. They won't know what hit them," Jessica said, wolfing down her lasagna.

"Dad, you've done a lot of good for people as a lawyer, with all your pro bono work," Elizabeth said. She picked up a leaf of lettuce with her fingers. "What do you think?"

Mr. Wakefield nodded with approval. "Well, I'm certainly an advocate of using the justice system when possible," he said slowly. "I think it's worth a try."

"Were you ever a lawyer in a case like this, Dad?" Jessica asked.

"Yes, I remember a case a few years back," he answered thoughtfully. "I defended a man who'd been wrongly accused of theft by the company he worked for. He lost his job. But we proved his innocence, and he was reinstated."

"We can't lose, Jess," Elizabeth said confidently as she poured herself a glass of ice water.

"Well, I said you girls should give it your best shot," Mr. Wakefield said cautiously. "But remember—you're facing a very powerful opposition."

Chapter 14

"What do you think you're doing alone in here?" Jessica demanded.

"It's my bedroom. It's probably legal for me to be alone in here," Elizabeth answered. She was lying on her bed, reading a book.

Jessica zipped up her black miniskirt. "But the basketball game is tonight."

"Well, I'm sure it will be exciting," Elizabeth said indifferently. She turned the page.

"What's the matter with you?" Jessica asked, sitting down on Elizabeth's bed. "You're acting like this is a morgue instead of a bedroom. I'd think you'd be ecstatic about your new SAT scores and ready to go out and have fun."

"I hadn't really planned to go to the game," Elizabeth said. She wasn't too thrilled about giving Todd yet one more chance to blow her off. "I'd rather be alone tonight. I have a lot to do."

"Like what? Shave your head and join a convent?"

"I see you're back to your old self," Elizabeth said, looking at Jessica over the top of her book. "I'm just not up to it. I tried to talk to Todd today, but I might as well have tried to hold a conversation with Prince Albert."

A car honked out in the driveway. Jessica leaped to the window above Elizabeth's desk and pushed aside the curtain.

"It's Ken!" she said. Then she went to the bed again and grabbed the book out of Elizabeth's hands.

"Hey, give that back. They're just about to confront the murderer," Elizabeth protested.

"You've got the rest of your life to read. The big game is *now*," Jessica said. "Never mind Todd. He'll be buried up to his neck in those boring college recruiters. Come with Ken and me."

"Jessica, hurry up! We'll miss the opening play!" Ken called from the driveway.

"It'll be fun," Jessica said, rummaging through Elizabeth's closet and pulling out a jean jacket. "Besides, Heather is probably licking her chops over the chance to take my place as head of the squad. I'll need all the help I can get to keep from gagging every time I look at her. If I'm lucky, she'll totally blow the solo cheer."

Elizabeth watched Jessica pull on the denim jacket. It looked great with her short skirt, black cowboy boots, and jangly silver earrings. Maybe if

Elizabeth threw on a nice outfit and went out, it would make her feel better.

So what if Todd would be too absorbed in the game and the talent scouts to bother waving to her from the court? She could still have fun.

Elizabeth sprang up and pulled her favorite jeans out of her bureau drawer. "Jessica, go get me your black low-necked T-shirt and hammered gold earrings," she instructed.

"Coming up," Jessica said with a grin.

"I've never seen people going this wild at a basketball game," Jessica said, clasping Ken's hand.

"I know, I can't believe how packed it is," Elizabeth agreed. "I can hardly hear myself think." Everyone in the stands was going nuts.

"I certainly didn't need to wear anything over my T-shirt," Jessica said. She pulled off Elizabeth's jean jacket. "It's so hot in here."

"It's like a jungle," Ken said. "Look, the team's coming out."

Ken applauded loudly as the Sweet Valley High basketball team ran out onto the court.

"We're gonna win!" a guy in the bleachers screamed.

Elizabeth looked up into the bleachers and saw Tim Nelson, Tad Johnson, Bryce Fisherman, and about ten other guys from the football team stamping their feet in the stands.

"Go, Gladiators!" Tad screamed.

At the side of the court, Annie, Sandy, and Jeanie were doing a routine of cartwheels and jumps. They also yelled out a cheer for each player coming onto the gymnasium floor.

Elizabeth searched the floor for Todd, but couldn't find him among the players practicing their layups and foul shots. Her heart pounded as she waited to catch a glimpse of him.

When Todd finally raced out, all of the spectators on Sweet Valley High's side of the gym shot to their feet, stamping and clapping.

"Todd! Todd! Todd!" a row of girls screamed.

Maria and Annie were leading the crowd in a special cheer for him. "S-I-N-K, sink it, Todd, sink it!" they screamed.

Despite herself, Elizabeth felt a tiny tug of pride that her boyfriend was such a big deal at Sweet Valley High.

Elizabeth noted that a bunch of guys in suits were sitting on a bench near the court. They were all wearing carnations in their lapels, and each of them held a clipboard and a pen. They had to be the college recruiters. Elizabeth felt a chill just watching them adjust their collars and write on their clipboards. She shook her head, realizing that Todd was dealing with megapressure.

Elizabeth felt a sudden pang of guilt that she'd asked him to take a break from practice earlier in the day to talk to her. Tonight was the biggest night of his life.

She watched Todd lean over to catch his breath. He looked tired. *I hope he'll be all right out there,* she thought.

"I'm glad you're here," Lila said. Jessica and Ken sat down next to her on the crowded bench. "I was afraid I was going to have to stomach Heather's strutting alone."

Heather strode out onto the floor and started off the next cheer with a no-handed cartwheel and a back flip.

"I'm already feeling a bit queasy," Jessica answered.

"Are you even allowed to be here?" Lila asked.

"What are they going to do, throw me out?" Jessica replied. "I wouldn't miss this game for anything—especially since I choreographed half the cheers."

"Well, I wish you were out there on the court and Heather was tied up in heavy traffic somewhere," Lila said, wrinkling her nose.

"I do deserve to be out there," Jessica said to Ken. He pulled her into a bear hug, and the strength of his arms was comforting.

"With any luck, you will be soon," Ken said. Driving over to the game, Jessica and Elizabeth had informed Ken about the plan for a mock trial.

"Thanks for coming by today," she said to him as he held her.

"Sometimes you have to fight for what's important," he whispered into her ear.

"The game must be starting in a minute," Jessica said. "Amy and Maria are lining up for the pregame cheering routine."

The whole squad walked to the center of the court and quickly spread out in formation. Then they flew into a Y-leap combination followed by two triple herkie's and a trojan jump.

Heather stepped forward for her solo cheer—the solo cheer Jessica had created.

"I didn't know they allowed dragons into public gymnasiums," Lila said dryly.

"Li, what do you think the chances are that Heather will mess up and make my day?" Jessica asked, feeling daggers of jealousy shoot from her eyes.

I hope Heather trips over her shoelaces, Jessica thought as she put her hand in her jeans pocket and crossed her fingers.

Heather leaped high into the air, flipping backward with a perfect landing. Then she flawlessly executed the rest of the routine.

Jessica felt her stomach cave in and slumped miserably against the hard bench. "She's really good, you know that, Ken? Heather is really good," Jessica said, shaking her head in despair.

Her self-esteem had climbed up to almost normal again after Ken had come by to see her, her parents had pledged their support, and Elizabeth had unveiled her plan. But now, watching Heather glide in and easily take her place on the squad, Jessica's self-worth took another nosedive.

"Maybe I don't deserve my cocaptain position back," Jessica said. "Maybe I've always kidded myself about how good I was, and how valuable I was to the squad."

"Heather looks good out there," Ken admitted. "But she's an ice princess. She does the moves all right, but there's something missing."

"There is?" Jessica asked hopefully.

Ken nodded. "She's technically perfect, but it's like she's out there to show off. It doesn't seem like she cares about inspiring the crowd and the players," Ken said. "Everyone is applauding Heather's performance, but do you see people really fired up and jumping to their feet?"

"No, I guess not," Jessica said, looking around the stands.

"No one can sit still when *you* do a solo cheer." He leaned over and gave her a kiss. "We need you back at school."

"I hope you're right," she said.

"I know I'm right," he replied softly. "And other people will know it, too."

"Everyone but you, Lila, and my sister want me to dig a hole to China and fall in," Jessica said sullenly.

"There'll be more than three of us behind you, Jess." Ken kissed her again. "I guarantee it."

The game was just beginning as Elizabeth wedged into a space on the bleachers between Enid and Olivia.

"We're playing against Palisades High," Enid said, pointing to the guys on the floor in orange-and-black uniforms.

"Uh-oh, that means it'll be a tough match," Olivia observed.

Two refs ran out to either end of the court and blew their whistles to start the game. Todd had the ball, and Palisades sent two six-foot-four guys out to guard him aggressively.

"They're going after Todd," Olivia said, taking off her sweatshirt.

Elizabeth watched Todd dart around the guards and dribble into center court. Everyone knew Todd was the best player of all the local high schools. It made sense that Palisades would direct its defense to interfere with him in any way possible. The two guards stayed inches from Todd as he thundered down the court, dribbling to the right, then left, to dodge them.

They're trying to wear him out, Elizabeth thought. She felt sad as she remembered the recruiters, who were surely recording Todd's every move on their clipboards.

"Looks like they're playing dirty," Enid said.

One of the guards elbowed Todd in the ribs, but the closest ref was so busy keeping an eye on the basket that he didn't see the foul. Todd winced but kept moving, keeping control of the ball. He leaped up under the basket for a layup shot.

"That's it, Todd!" Coach Tilman yelled from the bench. "Show 'em what you're made of!"

A Palisades player grabbed the ball and took off down the court with it. Then A. J. Morgan stole it and passed it to Todd, giving him a perfect open shot if he could reach the hoop from fifteen feet away. Todd flicked the ball and it sank neatly into the basket.

The Palisades players looked as if they were grinding their teeth with rage. Soon Todd was dribbling down the court again. A Palisades player grabbed him by the arm and the whistle blew.

"Foul!" yelled the referee.

"I think they're declaring war," Olivia said.

Elizabeth felt her heart pound.

Todd stepped to the foul line, took his shot, and scored. Jason Mann clapped him on the shoulder as he ran by. Just as A. J. got hold of the ball and passed it to Todd, a Palisades guy deliberately stuck his foot out, and Elizabeth gasped as Todd stumbled.

"How can they get away with that?" Elizabeth exclaimed furiously.

"The ref can only foul it if he sees it," Enid said.

Tom Hackett bounced a pass to Todd. But just as Todd reached for it, a player from Palisades checked him with his hip. Todd fell to the ground. Elizabeth's hands flew to her face. In a flash, Todd was on his feet again, apparently unhurt.

"Foul!" yelled the ref.

"They're trying to kill him out there!" Elizabeth said.

"Todd's pretty fast, he can handle them," Olivia reassured her. "Besides, look at all the foul shots he's getting."

Todd was dribbling expertly down the court, leaving his defense guards in the dust and dodging Palisades players at every step. Elizabeth glanced down at the recruiters and saw that none of them were writing on their clipboards. Their attention was riveted on Todd.

The players were only ten minutes into the game, and it looked as if Todd would take Sweet Valley to victory again.

He came in swiftly under the basket, raised his arms over his head, and leaped into the air for the layup. But as his feet left the ground, a Palisades player dived and pulled Todd's legs out from under him. The ball flew out of his hands and Todd came crashing down on the court.

Elizabeth gasped and her heart flew into her mouth. She stared in wide-eyed horror as Todd writhed on the ground, grasping his ankle in obvious pain.

Both refs ran out onto the court, blowing their whistles.

"Intentional foul!" a referee screamed. "You! You're thrown out of the game!" He was pointing his finger at the player who'd fouled Todd.

The Palisades player jogged off the court. Elizabeth saw him grin at another teammate, who smiled back and slapped his palm.

A. J. and Jason rushed toward Todd, and Elizabeth saw Todd's parents pushing their way through the crowded stands onto the court. She glanced over at the recruiters, who had all jumped up from their seats, set down their clipboards, and run out onto the court.

"I need a doctor over here!" Elizabeth heard Coach Tilman shout over the noise in the gymnasium.

Elizabeth felt the blood drain from her face.

"Enid, I've got to get down there," she said frantically.

"Just don't get trampled," Enid advised. "There are about a million sports fans in here, all going crazy at once."

Elizabeth started to make her way down the bleachers. "Excuse me, excuse me," she said breathlessly.

She pushed her way down to the gym floor just in time to see a doctor press through and kneel down next to Todd.

The doctor lightly touched Todd's ankle, and Todd let out a cry of pain.

"Just keep breathing," the doctor said calmly.

"That's my best player," Coach Tilman roared. "Can you get him fixed up?"

"What am I going to tell the basketball team back at Yale?" a recruiter asked anxiously.

The doctor shook his head. "It looks like this young man has fractured his right ankle. I'm afraid he might not play basketball again for a long, long time."

"Tough break," Elizabeth heard another one of the recruiters say. "We had a lot of hope for that kid. He would have been good on my team."

"Yeah, sorry it happened," a third scout said.

"Well, game's over for us, I guess. It was nice to meet you, Coach Tilman."

Elizabeth felt her heart break for Todd as the recruiters all sadly shook hands with Coach Tilman and left the gymnasium.

Paramedics were carrying Todd on a stretcher to a waiting ambulance. Elizabeth started to run after them. But then she stopped. She thought back to the last few times she'd tried to talk to him—in the cafeteria, at his house, at Miller's Point, outside the gym earlier that day.

He really doesn't need me. He's been making that pretty obvious. Maybe I should just face reality. Elizabeth turned around and climbed slowly back to her seat in the stands.

Chapter 15

"Are you sure this will work?" Jessica asked.

"You're not getting cold feet, are you?" Elizabeth said.

Elizabeth turned right at a stop sign and headed the Jeep toward Sweet Valley High. "I know it's scary, but there's no other choice. We just have to persuade the school to let you have a trial."

Jessica gazed out the window as the houses and lawns sped by. On Friday night, as she'd sat safely with her family and then snuggled in the warmth of Ken's arms, Jessica's whole body had been lit with excitement over the mock trial. But now, as she and Elizabeth drove to school on Monday morning, a feeling of dread crept up her spine.

"What if they say no?" Jessica asked.

"After we worked all weekend writing up a great proposal?" Elizabeth asked.

As Elizabeth turned into the school parking lot, Jessica's stomach began doing gymnastics. The boldness Jessica had felt at home that morning, as she'd dressed in her most elegant black skirt, maroon jacket, and velvet pumps, was disintegrating.

"Don't worry," Elizabeth continued. "They'll agree. It's only fair."

"This is the school board," Jessica said, slouching down in the seat. "They don't have to be fair."

"I guarantee you. Within three days the auditorium will be transformed into a courtroom," Elizabeth said. "And not only that, once we've got you back in school again, you'll probably get extra credit in every class for effort and ingenuity."

Trust Elizabeth to think about grades when Jessica's entire social life at Sweet Valley High was at stake. Everyone in school knew she'd been suspended. What would they say when they saw her in the halls? Would anyone be on her side?

Elizabeth parked the car and opened the door on the driver's side.

"Liz, I can't do this," Jessica said.

"You're scared to face Mr. Cooper?" Elizabeth said, getting her book bag out of the backseat.

"No, my ex-friends."

Elizabeth stopped rummaging through her bag and looked directly at Jessica. "Well, you've got me."

"Lizzie, what if we lose the trial and I end up more humiliated than I am now?" Jessica asked in a hoarse whisper.

"Jess, you're a fighter," Elizabeth said, gripping Jessica's shoulders. "And this is no time to lose your nerve. Now, walk into that school building like you own the place."

Jessica opened the Jeep door and stepped out onto the pavement. "You make me sound like a gunslinger."

"Well, pretend you're Annie Oakley," Elizabeth said. "Do whatever you need to do to feel brave. Let's go in."

Caroline Pearce began whispering to a cluster of people as Jessica and Elizabeth walked through the halls.

"I hate this," Jessica whispered.

"Ignore them," Elizabeth whispered back.

"Should I check into homeroom for old time's sake?" Jessica asked wryly.

"As my first official protest of your suspension, I'm blowing off homeroom completely," Elizabeth said.

"I like your style, Liz," Jessica grinned.

"It was a tough job, but I knew I'd get you to smile before we reached Chrome Dome's office," Elizabeth said.

Jessica marched purposefully next to Elizabeth, past rows of classrooms and banks of lockers.

"People are staring at me."

"Then stare back."

Jessica stopped in front of the main door to Mr. Cooper's office and took a deep breath.

"Ready for battle?" Elizabeth asked.

Jessica smoothed her skirt. "Ready."

She turned the brass knob and stepped with Elizabeth into the reception area, heading straight toward Chrome Dome's door.

"You can't go in there without an appointment," Rosemary said, jumping up from her typewriter. "Stop right now!"

Jessica and Elizabeth ignored the disgruntled secretary and stepped into Chrome Dome's office. He quickly stood up and whipped off his glasses.

"I have a summons for you, Mr. Cooper," Elizabeth said. She produced a sheaf of typed papers from her book bag. "Assuming it's agreeable to the administration, we wish to hold a mock trial for Jessica during Wednesday assembly."

"Just what is this?" Chrome Dome demanded.

"I'll represent Jessica in court," Elizabeth explained politely. "The details are outlined herein. Have a good day."

"Elizabeth, was I seeing things, or was that Jessica walking through the halls with you this morning?" Enid asked, crumbling saltine crackers into her vegetable soup.

Olivia was peeling an orange. "I thought she wasn't allowed within a continent of the school grounds."

Elizabeth unwrapped a tuna-fish sandwich. "She's not," she answered. "And the fact that she's not is a gross violation of justice. We've made our objections known to Mr. Cooper."

"Really?" Olivia asked wide-eyed.

"What did you do?" Enid whispered loudly.

A part-time secretary from Chrome Dome's office entered the cafeteria and strode over to the table. She tapped Elizabeth on the shoulder, handed her a note, and walked quickly away.

Elizabeth dropped her sandwich onto her plate as she read the note. Her heart leaped. *I have to call Jessica, we've got so much to do.*

"Is something wrong?" Enid asked.

"No, something is finally right," Elizabeth said, waving the note like a flag. "The school board has agreed to let us hold a mock trial for Jessica this Wednesday. We're going to prove her innocence, once and for all."

"Wow," Olivia said.

"But are you sure she didn't cheat?" Enid asked skeptically.

"Enid, would my sister care enough about a test to bother cheating?" Elizabeth said, picking up her sandwich and taking a bite.

"I see your point," Enid answered. She spooned up her soup.

"But the real point is that Jessica has had her life torn apart by a totally unfair accusation," Elizabeth declared loudly.

Students at the two nearest tables stopped their conversations, turned around, and stared at Elizabeth.

Elizabeth leaned earnestly toward Enid and Olivia. "We'll present our case to a jury of teachers

165

and students. Both we and Mr. Cooper will bring out witnesses to testify on Jessica's character and past performance."

"I'm already thinking about the layout of the special edition of *The Oracle* that will be *entirely* devoted to the trial," Olivia said. "You could write an opinion page for it, Liz."

"I could start writing that now. It's my opinion that people shouldn't be judged unfairly by surface appearances," Elizabeth declared.

A group of sophomores and juniors had got up from their lunches and come near the table to listen. Others joined them, until a small crowd had gathered around Elizabeth.

"I also think that someone who doesn't do well in school can still be very smart and very capable on standardized tests," Elizabeth said, now speaking directly to people surrounding her. "We'll prove that my sister didn't cheat on the SATs."

"Right, and my sheepdog plays bass in Jamie Peters's band," someone yelled. People laughed rudely.

Elizabeth twisted around to where the jeering voice had come from. "You have no understanding of what's really going on," she announced.

"I think Jessica's totally guilty," someone whispered.

"Yeah, she seems like the type to cheat on a test," another voice answered.

The people standing around Elizabeth continued murmuring to each other as they drifted back to their own tables.

Elizabeth sat down and picked up her sandwich, but realized she wasn't hungry anymore. Her father's words echoed in her ears. *You're facing a powerful opposition.*

She and Jessica had been granted their mock trial, but it was going to be a tough fight. Did they have the strength to win?

"It'll be a breeze," Jessica said as she and Lila lounged by the Wakefield pool on Monday afternoon.

Lila raised her face to the sun. "You really think you can win the trial?"

"Sure, Elizabeth's got it all figured out," Jessica said confidently. She lay back on a bright-yellow beach towel.

"Well, I considered it my civic duty to ditch afternoon classes as a way to show my support for you," Lila murmured, adjusting her sunglasses.

"Oh, absolutely." Jessica took a long drink from a glass of pink lemonade. Then she rolled over onto her stomach and pursed her lips. "Hey, Li, would you be on my jury?"

Lila pulled a bottle of coconut lotion out of her beach bag. "I'm not exactly an impartial party," she responded.

"But why can't I have my friends judge me?" Jessica demanded, propping her chin on her fists. "That doesn't seem fair."

"It might not be fair, but it's the way it's done in a court of law," Lila said. She squeezed oil onto her arms and legs and then offered the lotion to Jessica. "I don't mean to alarm you, but this whole business of a mock trial might not be a pothole-free road."

Jessica accepted the bottle from Lila and poured scented oil over her long, tan legs. She rubbed her smooth skin and then rolled over onto her back, feeling the hot, rejuvenating rays of the sun warm her body.

"Who cares what the road is like? I've got a Jeep," Jessica said casually.

"How silly of me," Lila replied.

"You should have seen Chrome Dome's face when we burst into his office." Jessica giggled. "He looked like he was about to blow a fuse."

"That man really needs to relax. You should've invited him to hang out by the pool with us," Lila said.

"Remind me not to let you plan my next party."

The portable phone rang and Jessica picked it up.

"This is Mr. Cooper," said the voice at the other end.

Jessica quickly cupped her hand over the receiver. "Lila, it's Chrome Dome," she whispered. Then she put the phone back to her ear.

"Hi, Mr. Cooper," Jessica said sweetly.

"Jessica, in light of recent developments, I'm suspending your suspension," Chrome Dome said. "We'll discuss the future on Wednesday afternoon."

"Thank you," Jessica said, lifting her eyebrows.

"In the meantime, you're expected at school in the morning," he said.

"I'll be there, sir," Jessica said seriously, making a face at Lila.

"And you can tell Ms. Fowler that we're expecting her, as well," Chrome Dome instructed.

The line went dead.

"What's all the commotion in front of the school?" Elizabeth asked.

"I don't know, it looks like a pep rally," Jessica said as she pulled the Jeep into the far end of the student parking lot on Tuesday morning.

"I didn't know there was a game tonight," Elizabeth said, frowning.

Elizabeth slung her purse over her shoulder, got out of the car, and glanced at her watch. "Come on, we don't want to be late for homeroom. You're better off not drawing attention to yourself on your first day back at school."

Jessica grabbed her books out of the backseat and walked quickly across the asphalt with Elizabeth.

Dana Larson came running toward them, wearing a T-shirt that said "We Believe in Jessica!" in bold black letters.

"You might want to stay out of the way of this," Dana said, catching her breath. "The junior class is split. Half are for you and half are against you, Jess."

"Half the class is *against* me? I *knew* I didn't want to face everyone in school," Jessica wailed.

Is it a big a mistake to have Jessica at school the day before the trial? Elizabeth wondered. What if her spirit was crushed too much for her to testify convincingly?

169

"Don't forget, a lot of people are for you," Dana said. "DeeDee made T-shirts for a bunch of us who are on your side." A small parade of students wearing the same T-shirt Dana had on were marching peacefully in a circle.

"We believe in Jessica!" the marchers chanted.

"It looks like the opposition may be stronger, though," Elizabeth said with alarm. On the other side of the school's concrete steps, Ron Edwards, Paul Sherwood, and Charlie Cashman were fiercely shaking their fists in the air.

"Guilty as charged, Wakefield!" Charlie yelled, looping his fingers around the silver buckles of his leather motorcycle jacket.

"Whose idea was it to rally against me?" Jessica cried angrily. "What kind of heartless jerk would organize this?"

A chill ran up Elizabeth's spine as she saw Bruce Patman step through the group of students who were screaming out against Jessica.

Bruce sauntered toward the twins, staring at Jessica with a murderous look on his face.

"Hey, Patman," Tad Johnson said, leaning against an iron stair rail and high-fiving Bruce.

Sashaying close behind Bruce was Heather Mallone, her face twisted into a cruel smirk.

"I should have known Heather would go for any trick that would keep me off the squad for good," Jessica said between clenched teeth.

Bruce walked up and stood inches from Jessica,

170

his arms folded across his "Jessica is Guilty" T-shirt.

"Nice T-shirt, Bruce," Jessica said coolly. "Now, back off. You're standing in my personal space."

"Don't you like the little party I've thrown for you?"

"I should have known you'd be the one responsible for this," Jessica said with narrowed eyes.

Jessica's voice was controlled, but Elizabeth could see that her sister's body was shaking.

"I'm going to teach you never to humiliate me in public again," Bruce hissed. "My rally will ruin any chance of your winning that trial." Then he turned and disappeared into the crowd.

Jessica stood with her chin held high, but her face was drained of all color.

"Never mind him," Elizabeth said quietly, placing a hand on Jessica's shoulder.

"It's all over, Liz," Jessica whispered, a single tear rolling down her ashen cheek. "Bruce is going to destroy me."

Just then Zack Johnson, Robbie Hendricks, and Scott Trost came charging around the corner with Tad, Bryce, Ricky, and Danny. They were all wearing T-shirts that said "We Believe in Jessica!"

"Jessica is innocent," their deep voices chanted.

Ken raced around the corner after them with Claire Middleton and Tim Nelson.

"Look!" Jessica screamed, drying her tears. "Ken is leading the Gladiators for us."

Ken jogged over, picked Jessica up in his arms, and held her tightly, giving her a long kiss. Then he set her back down on the ground and handed each twin her own "We believe in Jessica!" T-shirt.

"I told you there'd be more than three people behind you, Jess," Ken said. "And this isn't all." He cupped his hands to his mouth. "Now, Amy!" he shouted.

Amy ran out of the school building with the entire cheerleading squad—minus Heather.

"One, two, three!" Amy yelled. Then Annie, Amy, Maria, Jeanie, and Sandy cartwheeled, kicked, and leaped, screaming out their support for Jessica.

"Jessica Rules!" they cheered.

Then Amy climbed up on Annie's shoulders. With Jeanie and Sandy each holding one of her legs to steady her, Amy pulled out a banner that said "Jessica is Innocent." She held it high over her head.

"Jessica! Jessica!" Maria yelled, stamping her feet and clapping her hands in rhythm.

Amy tossed the banner out into the crowd, and Jeanie and Sandy helped her jump down to the ground. Then Amy ran up to Jessica and threw her arms around her.

"I finally came to my senses," Amy said. "We all talked it over and remembered how you'd stood up for Maria and Sandy when Heather kicked them off the squad. I'm so sorry, Jess." Amy hugged Jessica again. "You're a great friend. And I know you're innocent."

Elizabeth sighed with relief as Amy and the other cheerleaders all gathered around Jessica, hugging and crying.

As the crowd began to break up and people filtered into the school building, Elizabeth scanned the school yard for Todd. He was nowhere in sight.

"Jason, have you seen Todd? Do you know how he's doing?" Elizabeth asked.

"No," Jason said with a shrug. "I don't think any of the other guys on the team have talked to him since the game, either."

None of his teammates have bothered to check on him? Elizabeth thought. *Maybe he does need me, after all.*

"No thanks, Mom, I don't need anything," Todd called listlessly from his bed.

He kicked off his flannel comforter with his good leg, trying not to move the one in a cast. Halfheartedly, Todd picked up a copy of *Sports Illustrated,* then flung it back onto the bed. It was too depressing to read, especially if the stories had anything to do with basketball.

None of the college scouts had called since the game, and the steady flow of catalogs and scholarship offers had stopped. Coach Tilman had told him not to bother to come to practice, even to learn by watching from the bench. None of the guys from the basketball team had even come by to visit.

Todd's uncle had called the night before from northern California, and then his cousin had called from back east. But he wasn't in the mood to talk to anyone.

He lay still and stared around the room at his basketball plaques and trophies. Bronze statues of agile players leaping for the basket lined every bookshelf. His bedroom walls were cluttered with framed certificates naming Todd as most valuable player. Every award he'd won since eighth grade had now come to nothing.

Todd picked up his injured leg and adjusted it slightly on the bed. It was itchy and roasting from the heavy plaster that covered it from his ankle to his knee. But the rest of his body was cold and hollow with loneliness.

He wished Elizabeth would call.

He'd been such an egotistical creep to her, he wouldn't be surprised if she never wanted to speak to him again. Todd missed her so much, his chest ached. She was the one genuine thing in his life. Elizabeth loved him for who he was—whether or not he was a basketball star or a high scholastic achiever.

He covered his face with his hands, remembering how he'd treated her lately. How could he possibly have refused her the support she'd needed when she'd been really down about her first test scores? He could kick himself for not having told her that he knew she'd do better the second time. Now he'd probably destroyed their relationship.

I've got nothing left, he thought miserably. *My life is ruined.*

Todd slowly took his hands from his face and brushed away the tears. Then he heard a sound outside his room and weakly turned his head.

Elizabeth was standing in the doorway, with a beautiful smile on her face. Her sparkling blue eyes were filled with love and compassion.

"Elizabeth!" he cried with a rush of happiness. "I don't believe you're here," he said.

"I thought you could use a few things," she said cheerfully, stepping into the room.

She was holding a plate of homemade chocolate-chip cookies in one hand and a large shopping bag in the other.

"We didn't have any walnuts in the house," she apologized as she handed him the plate of cookies. "I hope you don't mind."

"I don't mind." He stared at her angelic face with disbelief.

Elizabeth perched on the bed and spilled the contents of the shopping bag onto the blankets.

"Well, let's see," Elizabeth said, surveying the items. "Felt-tipped pens, coloring books, blank paper, magazines, modeling clay. Looks like everything we'll need."

Todd leaned comfortably back on the pillows, so filled with love and gratitude for Elizabeth, he thought his heart would burst. The delicious aroma of the fresh-baked cookies floated warmly through the room.

"Elizabeth, I'm . . . I'm so sorry," Todd stammered.

"Just relax and enjoy the cookies while I concentrate," Elizabeth said gently. "I've come with great artistic purpose."

She uncapped a purple marker and began to draw on his cast. He laughed in spite of himself as Elizabeth decorated his plastered leg with blue, orange, green, yellow, and pink designs.

"Liz, I can't understand why you're being so nice to me after I've been such a jerk these past few weeks," Todd finally said.

Elizabeth stopped drawing and looked up at him.

"I know how it feels to have all confidence in yourself suddenly zapped." She placed a hand on his cheek. "But things will get better. You'll make it through this."

He clasped both her hands, and the markers spilled off the bed. He pulled her to him and kissed her deeply, holding her tighter than he ever had before. "I don't deserve you, Liz," he whispered hoarsely.

"Well, I'm not going to abandon you just because you were totally insufferable for a few weeks," she said, arching an eyebrow. "But you'd better not try that again!"

"I can't believe I almost lost you because of my arrogant pigheadedness." He held her close to him again and smelled the fresh scent of her hair. "I guess sometimes you have to hit bottom before you find out who your real friends are."

Chapter 16

"Come down for breakfast, girls," Mrs. Wakefield called.

"We've fixed hot pancakes. You'll need your strength for court this morning," Mr. Wakefield yelled.

"I'll be down in a minute!" Jessica shouted frantically from upstairs. "I can't decide what to wear." She pulled one top after another out of her closet. Was brown bold enough? Was red too bold? Jessica nervously twisted her hair around her fingers. Why couldn't she just throw on a blouse and skirt, wrap a scarf around her neck, and look great, as usual?

Would dress pants or a skirt give her more credibility? Should she wear makeup? She stared at herself in the small mirror above her bureau and pulled her hair up on top of her head with one hand. Would she look more sophisticated with a bun?

Jessica let her hair drop back onto her shoulders and sighed in frustration.

"Front and center," Mrs. Wakefield called again. "You have to be out of the house in twenty minutes, and I want you to eat something first."

"Coming!" Jessica yelled.

She grabbed a top and skirt off their hangers and stuck her feet into a pair of sandals. Hopping into her skirt in the hallway, she pulled the shirt over her head on the way down the stairs. Her head popped through the top of the shirt just in time to avoid a collision with her sister.

Elizabeth was crawling around on her hands and knees, peering under furniture with a wild look in her eyes.

"What are you looking for, Sherlock?" Jessica said as she pulled a comb through her hair.

"My briefcase with my notes! I've looked everywhere. I just had it last night. I can't believe I—" Elizabeth sputtered, looking up. "Nice outfit, Jess. If you show up in court like that, they won't merely suspend you, they'll toss you into the loony bin."

"What do you mean?" Jessica said defensively, glancing down at her clothes.

She saw that she had on an electric-orange shirt with a ruffled collar, which totally clashed with her bright-red flared skirt.

"Aaaargh!" Jessica groaned. "I'm not going to survive this day!" She ran back upstairs to put on something sane.

When Jessica walked back into the kitchen, she was wearing a blue silk top and a black linen skirt. Elizabeth was slamming cabinet doors and rifling crazily through the broom closet.

"Looking for this?" Mrs. Wakefield asked, dangling a black briefcase by its handle.

"Thanks, Mom." Elizabeth took the case. "I'm a little stressed-out this morning." She tripped over the legs of her chair and fell into the seat.

"I thought there might be a case of nerves around here," Mr. Wakefield said calmly. "Jess, take some pancakes, bacon, and cantaloupe. Then pass them."

"We have to succeed today," Elizabeth said, serving herself two blueberry pancakes and a spoonful of melon. "The school board can't be allowed to twist the truth just because they have the authority to do it. I have to *prove* that they can't."

Jessica poured maple syrup onto her pancakes and watched the thick liquid pooling at the edges of her plate. Elizabeth was all fired up about being a lawyer and seeing justice done, but Jessica was the one on trial. Her whole life was at stake.

"I've got something to prove, too," Jessica said, pushing pancake pieces around in the syrup with her fork. "I need to convince a jury that I really am smart enough to have got those scores on my own. If they don't believe that, they'll nail me for cheating, for sure."

Elizabeth's heart sank when she walked into Sweet Valley High and saw people pacing the halls

179

with picket signs that said "Jessica Is Guilty."

But Lila and Olivia were pinning a huge purple banner across the hall ceiling that said "Jessica Is Innocent!"

"This is great, you guys," Elizabeth said gratefully.

"You're going to win, Liz," Lila responded, giving Elizabeth a thumbs-up.

Elizabeth's heart skipped a beat when she caught sight of Todd, standing on his crutches in the hallway, talking to Ken.

"Care to sign our petition?" Ken asked.

He handed Elizabeth a piece of paper loaded with signatures. Her eyes filled with tears as she read the sentences at the top of the page: "We, the undersigned, do hereby believe that Jessica Wakefield is innocent. We fully support her unconditional return to Sweet Valley High."

"Yes, I will sign your petition."

Elizabeth signed her name and then looked up into Ken and Todd's hopeful faces. She patted her briefcase. "Well, wish me luck."

Students were filing noisily into the auditorium and clamoring to get seats up front. Chairs had been set up on the stage for the jury, witnesses, and defendent. Student technicians were busy hooking up cables for an onstage microphone; someone else was carrying a large oak desk onto the stage for the judge.

Elizabeth was too nervous to sit. She stood in the back of the auditorium, reading through her notes again.

It seemed like centuries ago when Elizabeth had felt that the most important thing in the world was doing well on the SATs. She wanted to win the case today, but she wasn't even thinking about her own success. The only thing that mattered was Jessica.

Mr. Cooper rose from his seat, walked onto the stage, and stepped up to the podium. The room quieted. Elizabeth squeezed her eyes shut and tried to send her twin a psychic message. *We can do it, Jess. We're prepared for anything.*

"Good morning, everyone," Mr. Cooper said into the microphone. "We're here today for the trial of Jessica Wakefield, who has been charged by the school board with cheating on the SATs. Elizabeth Wakefield will serve as Jessica's counsel. I will speak for the school board. I'd like to call the jury to their seats."

Six students from the junior and senior class and six teachers filed onto the stage and sat in their assigned chairs. Elizabeth had double-checked to be sure no one selected for the jury knew Jessica very well, so they wouldn't be prejudiced in their judgment.

"And will the judge please step up?"

Mrs. Jefferson, the school librarian, walked onto the stage and sat down behind the desk. Elizabeth had always liked her; they talked a lot about literature and history. Mrs. Jefferson had strong opinions about truth and justice.

Mrs. Jefferson smoothed her gray hair and straightened out the sleeves of her tailored suit. Then she picked up the wooden gavel from the desk and tapped it lightly on the table. Chrome Dome jumped at the noise.

"Mrs. Jefferson, is everything all right?" he asked.

"Everything is fine, Mr. Cooper," she answered crisply. "Just making sure the equipment works."

"Yes, well, let's begin. Elizabeth, please come to the stage for your opening statement."

The butterflies that had been nestled in Elizabeth's stomach took flight. She took a deep breath and walked slowly onto the stage, her knees shaking as she approached the podium.

In the audience Mr. Collins flashed Elizabeth a thumbs-up. She smiled back at him and felt her body flood with a warm sensation of courage. She adjusted the microphone and spread out the pages of her speech.

"What is at stake here today is the future of one human being—my sister, Jessica Wakefield. But what is also at stake is truth itself. The school board has arbitrarily accused Jessica of cheating based on what they believe is her complete record. I intend to prove that their evidence, and therefore their interpretation, is quite incomplete," Elizabeth began.

Murmurs rose and fell in the audience. Elizabeth took a sip from the glass of water provided for her.

"Jessica's academic record may not match the typical profile of a person who would score high on the SATs, but, in fact, she's extremely intelligent. She's smart enough to have aced the tests without cheating," Elizabeth said passionately. "She's definitely different from what the school board expects her to be. But she has a right to be different."

People in the audience were nodding their heads.

"People are very complex," Elizabeth continued. "They're not always what they seem to be on the surface. We should be careful about how we judge one another, and how we might narrow-mindedly believe we know the depth of a person's capabilities. My sister is innocent. The truth of that will become clear."

Elizabeth put her papers back in their folder and swiftly walked back to take her seat in the front row of the auditorium. As she passed the spot where her sister was sitting at the edge of the stage, Jessica quickly reached out and squeezed Elizabeth's hand.

"The school board has sent me a most interesting letter," Mr. Cooper began. "I would like to share it with all of you." He took off his glasses and polished them on his handkerchief.

He dramatically produced a letter from his coat pocket and proceeded to read.

To the Principal's Office
of Sweet Valley High:

In keeping with our general policy, we have checked records for each member of the junior and senior classes to compare grades, attitude, and attendance with SAT scores. This is done for the purpose of accruing statistics on education in our school district.

183

We are appalled by the record we've un-covered for Ms. Jessica Wakefield.

She's repeatedly received average grades—that is, when she's bothered to come to class. Our research indicates that she's consistently skipped classes one out of five days each week since she entered Sweet Valley High. And as for her attitude, we need only quote to you from several of her teachers:

"Sloppy, uninspired, and indifferent . . ."

"The rare assignments Jessica has turned in look as if the dog walked all over them. . . ."

"Jessica doesn't seem to care about her schoolwork at all. She has turned in only one out of six assigned reports—and that was on a subject matter having nothing to do with our current class work. . . ."

After examining her complete record, we were quite suspicious of Ms. Wakefield's ex-tremely impressive showing on the first SATs. Her poor scores on the retake have convinced us that she cheated on the first test. The board calls for her suspension for the rest of the school year.

Sincerely,
The School Board

Chrome Dome leaned over the podium as the au-dience whispered and shifted restlessly.

"This letter alone should be sufficient evidence

to—" he began, waving the paper over his head.

The wooden gavel banged on the oak desk with a loud crack. Chrome Dome nearly jumped out of his skin.

"This is speculation, Mr. Cooper," Mrs. Jefferson said dryly. "I'd like to proceed to the witnesses."

"Witnesses, yes, of course," Mr. Cooper mumbled. "We shall now proceed to the witnesses," he announced into the microphone, moving quickly off the stage.

Jessica sighed deeply. How could they possibly win this trial?

But what if they did win? she thought with alarm. Did her teachers really think she was sloppy, uninspired, and indifferent? Jessica had always believed her sole mission in life was to get away with doing as little as possible in school and acting as if she didn't care.

Maybe she just never believed she could do a better job.

It was hard for Jessica to imagine adjusting her priorities of fashion, suntanning, and guys. But maybe she should—just a little bit—if she ever survived this trial.

"Before I bring out the witnesses for the defense, I have some surprising evidence that may interest all of you," Elizabeth said from the podium. "The school board claimed in the letter you just heard that they examined Jessica's complete record. But there's a lot they don't know about her."

185

Elizabeth opened up her folder and pulled out a set of papers. Someone coughed in the back of the auditorium, and the sound echoed throughout the room. Elizabeth's heart pounded; she could feel that her palms were damp. Finally, she stood up straight and held the papers high in her hand.

"I have here copies of all of Jessica's standardized tests from first grade on," Elizabeth said. "Every single score is exceptionally high." Gasps of shock escaped from the audience. "As you listen to the testimony of each of my witnesses, you'll begin to see that we should not judge the book of Jessica Wakefield by its cover. Mr. Jaworski, please come to the stand."

Mr. Jaworski, Sweet Valley's history teacher and drama coach, rose from his seat and stood at the microphone, next to Elizabeth.

"Jessica has been a student in my drama class and performed in the plays I've directed for the last three years," Mr. Jaworski said.

"And how has she been in class and performances?" Elizabeth asked, taking notes.

"Well, I admit that Jessica has not always been as prepared for the classroom and rehearsals as I would prefer," Mr. Jaworski said. "But she understands drama with greater depth and sophistication than any student I've ever seen. I believe that if she applied herself, she could become a brilliant actress."

Elizabeth's next witness was Nora Dalton.

"Ms. Dalton, tell us how you know Jessica," Elizabeth said.

"Jessica is a student in my French class," Ms. Dalton said into the microphone, lightly touching her straight black hair. "She always speaks perfectly when called on in class. I realized early on that Jessica instantly grasped each lesson in French grammar, then quickly became bored with the homework drills. She's a very bright girl, though she does tend to neglect turning in assignments."

"Thank you, Ms. Dalton," Elizabeth said.

Ms. Dalton smiled graciously, with a sparkle in her bright hazel eyes, and returned to her seat.

"I would like to call one final witness for the defense. Unfortunately, we didn't have time to speak with her before the trial, but I'm sure she'll cooperate. Heather Mallone, please come to the stand."

Heather bolted upright in her auditorium seat between Bruce Patman and Charlie Cashman. "No," she said firmly.

The gavel clacked.

"Ms. Mallone," Mrs. Jefferson said, "you've been called as a witness. You may not withhold information that may be pertinent to the case."

Heather reluctantly pushed herself up out of her seat, fuming. She stared hatefully at Jessica as she stalked up to the stage.

"Heather," Elizabeth said. "Tell us what Jessica is like as a cheerleader."

Heather squirmed uncomfortably at the podium.

"Ms. Mallone, this court hasn't got all day," Mrs. Jefferson said, drumming her fingers on the desk. "I will remind you that you are under oath to tell the truth."

"All right," Heather said, gritting her teeth. "Jessica . . . is an excellent cheerleader."

"Mmmm, I see," Elizabeth said thoughtfully. "And what can you say in regard to her intelligence?"

"I admit," Heather muttered, "that Jessica has outwitted me on more than one occasion."

Elizabeth nodded, keeping her face expressionless. *This is great!* she thought to herself.

Heather was obviously referring to the time she'd tried to steal the captain position of the cheerleading squad from Jessica. She'd attempted to buy the loyalty of the squad with gifts and dinner parties and promises of fame in the national competitions. Jessica had seen through Heather's ambitious manipulations before anyone else had.

"And I guess there's one other thing," Heather continued, frowning. "There's a rare spark to Jessica's intelligence. I see it in the way she choreographs cheers and teaches them to other people. I haven't often seen that kind of sharpness on a squad." She glared at Jessica. "And at my other school I worked with some of the very *best* cheerleaders in the country," Heather added, haughtily tossing her hair.

"Thank you, Heather," Elizabeth said, noting that the jury was gazing at Jessica with admiration. "You may step down."

A steaming-mad Heather stormed off the stage, and Elizabeth triumphantly returned to her seat.

Mr. Cooper stepped up to the microphone. "I'd now like to call the witnesses for the prosecution."

Elizabeth felt confident that Mr. Cooper's witnesses couldn't possibly say anything to take away from the strength of the defense. Still, she couldn't ignore the slight shaking of her hands.

Ms. Rice, the health teacher, came to the stand and said she'd never seen a student who paid attention less, and chattered and passed notes more. Mr. Frankel, the math teacher, said Jessica had turned in only three assignments all semester.

"I think she could be an excellent math student," Mr. Frankel added, "if she only applied herself."

"Thank you, Mr. Frankel. Now let's move to our final witness," Chrome Dome said quickly.

Mr. Archer, the biology teacher, walked up to the podium. "I have to admit that on our class field trips to the beach, Jessica has always goofed off," Mr. Archer said. "I'm not sure if her data on some of the marine experiments were actually her own, or someone else's."

"Then, Mr. Archer," Mr. Cooper said, leaning close to the witness, "do you believe that Jessica could have been capable of cheating on the SATs?"

"Objection!" Elizabeth said, leaping to her feet. "The prosecution is leading the witness!"

"I will allow this line of questioning, Elizabeth," Mrs. Jefferson said gently. "Teachers' impressions of Jessica, based on her past performance, are an important part of the evidence in this trial."

"Well," Mr. Archer said, shifting in his seat, "yes, I suppose it's possible. . . ."

A loud murmur swept the room. The twelve jury members were frowning and shaking their heads. Everyone in the audience was talking at once. Elizabeth's hopes were dashed. She looked onto the stage at Jessica, who was staring at her with fearful blue eyes.

A loud bang of the gavel silenced the commotion in the room. "We will recess for a short break," Mrs. Jefferson said, "and then return for the final testimony and the defense's closing remarks."

The trial was almost over. The only thing left was for Elizabeth to put her sister on the stand. And when Jessica got up there, it had better be good.

Chapter 17

As people walked back into the auditorium and returned to their seats, Jessica ran her fingers through her hair nervously. Her uneasiness grew as she watched Elizabeth walk up to the podium. *Relax,* Jessica thought, closing her eyes. *Just relax and be yourself.*

"I'd like to call the defendant, Jessica Wakefield, to the stand," Elizabeth said.

Jessica rose to her feet and held her head high. She knew she looked elegant in her simple cobalt-blue silk top, black skirt, and black pumps. She walked steadfastly up to the podium, blinking in the bright white of the stage lights. She looked out at the vast sea of people, all waiting expectantly for her to speak.

Well, this isn't as much fun as accepting an Academy Award, she thought, *but I guess it's good practice.*

"Hi, everyone," Jessica began softly. She was able to speak without a single tremor, and hearing the calmness in her own voice helped her feel bolder. "I've never seen the auditorium so packed. But, as most of you know, I always love a big party."

People laughed, and Jessica felt the tension in the audience relax slightly. She ran a hand delicately across her satin blond hair and looked around the room with a smile.

"There's been a lot of talk about attitude this morning—mine, as a matter of fact," Jessica said wryly. The audience chuckled lightly. "But I learned something important about attitude from taking the SATs twice," she added with great sincerity.

"The first time I took the test, I had a relaxed attitude. I'd gone to bed early and got a good night's rest. I wasn't at all worried. I got good scores. But the second time I took the exam, I was out of my mind with worry. I exhausted myself studying and even stayed up poring over my SAT workbooks all night before the test." Jessica paused for a sip of water. "And it's common knowledge that I blew the second exam."

She noticed that she had the rapt attention of everyone in the room.

"I admit that I was rather taken by surprise when Mr. Cooper first called me into his office to say the school board had accused me of cheating. I have just one thing to say to you, Mr. Cooper," Jessica said, gazing serenely down at Chrome

Dome. "I love the art on your walls, but I think you need some plants."

A loud snicker escaped the audience, and muffled laughter rippled like a wave through the room. Even Chrome Dome was unable to stop the corners of his mouth from curving up.

"But seriously, everyone," Jessica said, looking back out at the audience. "I have something else to say to all of you, including Mr. Cooper. Maybe I'm not really cut out for rigorous academics, like my sister, and like most people who score high on the SATs. A lot of you know me as a fashion hound, a would-be actress, a wild partyer . . ."

There was a hoot from a guy in the room, which made everyone else laugh.

". . . a goof-off," Jessica continued, grinning. "And, yes, these things are definitely part of the real me."

Jessica heard Lila laugh in the back of the auditorium, which infected the rest of her row with giggles.

"But with the help of my family, in particular my sister, Elizabeth, I've realized that I'm also smart— something I was never too sure of before. And being smart is also the real me."

Jessica paused and looked out at the sober, sympathetic faces watching her. She glanced back at Mrs. Jefferson.

"Go on, dear, we're all listening," Mrs. Jefferson said.

Jessica faced her audience again and rested her hands on the sides of the podium. "I didn't cheat on the SATs. I earned my scores fair and square. I hope you'll all believe me."

Todd watched Elizabeth walk up to the stage to make her closing statement. She stood with dignity, beautiful under the spotlight, and laid out her notes on the podium.

"Jessica has told you that she took her two SAT tests with very different attitudes and got very different scores. I'd like to close by discussing my own test scores, which actually fluctuated as wildly as Jessica's," Elizabeth said. "I scored in the seven hundreds on both sections on my second test, which some of you know." She took a deep breath. "But the first time I took the SATs, I scored in the four hundreds on both sections, which almost none of you knew."

A collective gasp rose from the audience.

Todd dropped his head and felt knots of regret bunch up in his stomach. He'd known her first scores; he was probably the only friend she'd told. He'd been so full of his own fleeting success that he'd paid no attention to how much she must have needed him. Yet Elizabeth had forgiven him.

"I unwittingly conducted an experiment," Elizabeth was saying. Todd lifted his head. "Jessica and I switched the conditions under which each of us took the test each time. Our scores reflected that. But no one accused me of cheating. I ask the jury to put themselves in Jessica's place. What if no one believed you could do well on the SATs—even if your twin sister did well?"

Elizabeth quietly scanned the audience. Then she put her notes back into a folder and placed them under her arm. "The defense rests."

The jury filed out, and Elizabeth and Jessica hugged their parents, who were waiting at the side of the stage.

"Elizabeth," Todd called to her. She turned her head. Her face brightened when she saw him, and she hurried over to where he stood, leaning on his crutches. He gave her a tender kiss.

"I'm so proud of you, Elizabeth," Todd said hoarsely.

She smiled. "It means a lot to me to hear you say that."

Fifteen minutes later the jury filed back into the auditorium.

Whatever they decided, it sure didn't take long, Jessica thought nervously.

One of the jury members walked over to the judge and handed her a piece of paper. Jessica's heart pounded as Mrs. Jefferson silently read the note.

"The decision is in," Mrs. Jefferson said. She set the paper down and folded her hands on the desk. "The jury finds Jessica not guilty."

Jessica's eyes widened.

"She's not to be penalized for any tests she missed during her suspension," Mrs. Jefferson continued.

"And Mr. Cooper is now obligated to fight on her behalf before the school board."

Mr. Cooper stepped up to the podium. "I have just one thing to say to you, Jessica Wakefield," he began seriously. Then the corners of his mouth curled up. "I had no idea there were students at this school with such wit and intelligence—and so much promise for the future. My task of defending you to the board won't be difficult."

Applause and cheering filled the auditorium. "Jessica, is there anything else you'd like to say?" Mr. Cooper asked over the din.

Jessica jumped up and took the microphone. "I'd like to thank my sister—the most intelligent person I've ever known."

Jessica climbed off the stage and wrapped Elizabeth in a huge hug.

"I'm sorry to say it looks like you'll be completely reinstated in school," Elizabeth said breathlessly.

"Well, I guess it won't be so bad," Jessica said. "Now that I know I could do well if I wanted to."

But now it was time to focus on what was really important: the fact that she and Elizabeth were headed for a visit to Sweet Valley University to see Steven. The trip would include spending money that Mr. Wakefield had promised them, lots of partying, and—best of all—missing school.

"Sweet Valley University, get ready to meet the one and only Jessica Wakefield!" she said aloud.

Jessica saw her sister raise her eyebrows. "Why do I have a feeling the trip is going to be more than I can handle?" Elizabeth asked.

Jessica grinned. "Carpe diem, Lizzie. Seize the day!"

Jessica and Elizabeth are heading for Sweet Valley University. When Jessica falls for an older guy, how far will she go to keep him?

Don't miss Sweet Valley High #118, **COLLEGE WEEKEND.**

Bantam Books in the Sweet Valley High series
Ask your bookseller for the books you have missed

#1	DOUBLE LOVE	#42	CAUGHT IN THE MIDDLE
#2	SECRETS	#43	HARD CHOICES
#3	PLAYING WITH FIRE	#44	PRETENSES
#4	POWER PLAY	#45	FAMILY SECRETS
#5	ALL NIGHT LONG	#46	DECISIONS
#6	DANGEROUS LOVE	#47	TROUBLEMAKER
#7	DEAR SISTER	#48	SLAM BOOK FEVER
#8	HEARTBREAKER	#49	PLAYING FOR KEEPS
#9	RACING HEARTS	#50	OUT OF REACH
#10	WRONG KIND OF GIRL	#51	AGAINST THE ODDS
#11	TOO GOOD TO BE TRUE	#52	WHITE LIES
#12	WHEN LOVE DIES	#53	SECOND CHANCE
#13	KIDNAPPED!	#54	TWO-BOY WEEKEND
#14	DECEPTIONS	#55	PERFECT SHOT
#15	PROMISES	#56	LOST AT SEA
#16	RAGS TO RICHES	#57	TEACHER CRUSH
#17	LOVE LETTERS	#58	BROKENHEARTED
#18	HEAD OVER HEELS	#59	IN LOVE AGAIN
#19	SHOWDOWN	#60	THAT FATAL NIGHT
#20	CRASH LANDING!	#61	BOY TROUBLE
#21	RUNAWAY	#62	WHO'S WHO?
#22	TOO MUCH IN LOVE	#63	THE NEW ELIZABETH
#23	SAY GOODBYE	#64	THE GHOST OF TRICIA
#24	MEMORIES		MARTIN
#25	NOWHERE TO RUN	#65	TROUBLE AT HOME
#26	HOSTAGE	#66	WHO'S TO BLAME?
#27	LOVESTRUCK	#67	THE PARENT PLOT
#28	ALONE IN THE CROWD	#68	THE LOVE BET
#29	BITTER RIVALS	#69	FRIEND AGAINST FRIEND
#30	JEALOUS LIES	#70	MS. QUARTERBACK
#31	TAKING SIDES	#71	STARRING JESSICA!
#32	THE NEW JESSICA	#72	ROCK STAR'S GIRL
#33	STARTING OVER	#73	REGINA'S LEGACY
#34	FORBIDDEN LOVE	#74	THE PERFECT GIRL
#35	OUT OF CONTROL	#75	AMY'S TRUE LOVE
#36	LAST CHANCE	#76	MISS TEEN SWEET VALLEY
#37	RUMORS	#77	CHEATING TO WIN
#38	LEAVING HOME	#78	THE DATING GAME
#39	SECRET ADMIRER	#79	THE LONG-LOST BROTHER
#40	ON THE EDGE	#80	THE GIRL THEY BOTH LOVED
#41	OUTCAST	#81	ROSA'S LIE

#82	KIDNAPPED BY THE CULT!	#102	ALMOST MARRIED
#83	STEVEN'S BRIDE	#103	OPERATION LOVE MATCH
#84	THE STOLEN DIARY	#104	LOVE AND DEATH IN LONDON
#85	SOAP STAR	#105	A DATE WITH A WEREWOLF
#86	JESSICA AGAINST BRUCE	#106	BEWARE THE WOLFMAN (SUPER THRILLER)
#87	MY BEST FRIEND'S BOYFRIEND	#107	JESSICA'S SECRET LOVE
#88	LOVE LETTERS FOR SALE	#108	LEFT AT THE ALTAR
#89	ELIZABETH BETRAYED	#109	DOUBLE-CROSSED
#90	DON'T GO HOME WITH JOHN	#110	DEATH THREAT
#91	IN LOVE WITH A PRINCE	#111	A DEADLY CHRISTMAS (SUPER THRILLER)
#92	SHE'S NOT WHAT SHE SEEMS	#112	JESSICA QUITS THE SQUAD
#93	STEPSISTERS	#113	THE POM-POM WARS
#94	ARE WE IN LOVE?	#114	"V" FOR VICTORY
#95	THE MORNING AFTER	#115	THE TREASURE OF DEATH VALLEY
#96	THE ARREST	#116	NIGHTMARE IN DEATH VALLEY
#97	THE VERDICT	#117	JESSICA THE GENIUS
#98	THE WEDDING		
#99	BEWARE THE BABY-SITTER		
#100	THE EVIL TWIN (MAGNA)		
#101	THE BOYFRIEND WAR		

SUPER EDITIONS:
PERFECT SUMMER
SPECIAL CHRISTMAS
SPRING BREAK
MALIBU SUMMER
WINTER CARNIVAL
SPRING FEVER

SUPER THRILLERS:
DOUBLE JEOPARDY
ON THE RUN
NO PLACE TO HIDE
DEADLY SUMMER
MURDER ON THE LINE
BEWARE THE WOLFMAN
A DEADLY CHRISTMAS
MURDER IN PARADISE
A STRANGER IN THE HOUSE
A KILLER ON BOARD

SUPER STARS:
LILA'S STORY
BRUCE'S STORY
ENID'S STORY
OLIVIA'S STORY
TODD'S STORY

MAGNA EDITIONS:
THE WAKEFIELDS OF SWEET VALLEY
THE WAKEFIELD LEGACY: THE UNTOLD STORY
A NIGHT TO REMEMBER
THE EVIL TWIN
ELIZABETH'S SECRET DIARY
JESSICA'S SECRET DIARY

SIGN UP FOR THE SWEET VALLEY HIGH® FAN CLUB!

Hey, girls! Get all the gossip on Sweet Valley High's® most popular teenagers when you join our fantastic Fan Club! As a member, you'll get all of this really cool stuff:

- Membership Card with your own personal Fan Club ID number
- A Sweet Valley High® Secret Treasure Box
- Sweet Valley High® Stationery
- Official Fan Club Pencil (for secret note writing!)
- Three Bookmarks
- A "Members Only" Door Hanger
- Two Skeins of J. & P. Coats® Embroidery Floss with flower barrette instruction leaflet
- Two editions of *The Oracle* newsletter
- Plus exclusive Sweet Valley High® product offers, special savings, contests, and much more!

Be the first to find out what Jessica & Elizabeth Wakefield are up to by joining the Sweet Valley High® Fan Club for the one-year membership fee of only $6.25 each for U.S. residents, $8.25 for Canadian residents (U.S. currency). Includes shipping & handling.

Send a check or money order (do not send cash) made payable to "Sweet Valley High® Fan Club" along with this form to:

SWEET VALLEY HIGH® FAN CLUB, BOX 3919-B, SCHAUMBURG, IL 60168-3919

NAME _____
(Please print clearly)

ADDRESS _____

CITY _____ STATE _____ ZIP _____
(Required)

AGE _____ BIRTHDAY _____ / _____ / _____

Offer good while supplies last. Allow 6-8 weeks after check clearance for delivery. Addresses without ZIP codes cannot be honored. Offer good in USA & Canada only. Void where prohibited by law.
©1993 by Francine Pascal   LCI-1383-123

Songs from the Hit TV Series

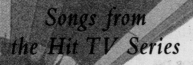

Featuring:

"Rose Colored Glasses"

"Lotion"

"Sweet Valley High Theme"

Available on CD and Cassette Wherever Music is Sold.